# Mary Wine

# Alcandian Rage

ELLORA'S CAVE
ROMANTICA PUBLISHING

An Ellora's Cave Romantica Publication

www.ellorascave.com

Alcandian Rage

ISBN 9781419954061
ALL RIGHTS RESERVED.
Alcandian Rage Copyright © 2005 Mary Wine
Edited by Sue-Ellen Gower
Cover art by Syneca

This book printed in the U.S.A. by Jasmine–Jade Enterprises, LLC.

Electronic book Publication September 2005

# ALCANDIAN RAGE

ꜱꜱ

# Chapter One
*Earth*

ৰ০

"You should eat."

Zeva moved her eyes around to the doorway but only out of curiosity. A female voice was foreign to her captivity and the one coming from the doorway rated a look. Her abandoned food tray wasn't worth considering. Zeva needed her body in top form and her limited exercise periods meant she had to control her caloric intake to avoid gaining weight.

Besides, she refused to be predictable like some animal in a zoo that had long ago forgotten that it was a captive.

"I am Cassandra." Zeva controlled her urge to smile sarcastically at the female guard. The clothing she wore was the fabric Zeva had come to recognize as Earth's military uniform. It was misshapen splotches of green, brown and beige. This Cassandra wore a pair of pants decorated in those splotches and a green shirt of the same fabric. Zeva detested the uniform. It drove home her state of captivity. It was amazing how you took for granted all of the little things in life that made you look forward to the next sunrise.

Things like, being surrounded by people that you did not need to hide your smiles from. Here on Earth, Zeva had to tighten her attention and capture any little emotional display. The guards around her delighted in recording any and all things she did. Their security cameras never turned away from her.

Cassandra walked into the room. Zeva watched the way she moved because her black boots did not make a sound on the smooth tile. That was a skill she could respect. It spoke of a female who valued training and Zeva understood that.

"If you could tell me what food you prefer, I will make certain your meals are more to your taste." Cassandra looked at the dark stain of sweat marking the Alcandian girl's T-shirt. Her breathing had calmed now but she had been working out in the containment cell when Cassandra entered.

Cassandra held a secret admiration for her. Zeva, she corrected herself. This woman might be an alien but she was a person. It was strange how a little knowledge could change your outlook on life. Like most humans, Cassandra had not been in the loop as far as information went on Earth's contact with Alcandar.

Cassandra grimaced. Well, it was a past association with the other planet now. The Alcandian girl in front of her was the only thing left of that relationship.

"You can watch me through your television cameras just as well." Zeva pointed out that fact as she moved her feet into a better stance. Knowing she was being watched every second of the day and night was one thing, having her jailer in the same room was more than her temper wanted to tolerate.

Zeva frowned at her own thoughts. What exactly was she going to do? She was trapped in the room and any demonstrations of her anger on her pathetic jailers got her confined to a much smaller cell. They called it discipline—she had other names for it. Ones her mother would have scolded her for using.

"Sorry. I shouldn't have stared at you."

Zeva lifted an eyebrow. Now that was different. Courtesy from a human was indeed a rarity. This human had light-colored hair. Blonde, they called it. Her eyes were the same blue as Jessica's brother too.

"I came to see if you are interested in working. Command has decided to offer you a job. It isn't very interesting work but I guess it would beat this room."

That would not be hard to do. Zeva studied the woman a moment. "What kind of job?"

"Uniform warehousing. It's boring work and the warehouse is always too hot or cold. You do a lot of lifting and walking. Of course York told me to warn you that if you tell anyone who you are—"

Zeva snorted, cutting Cassandra off. "He will what? I will tell you what he will do...nothing! This York is a coward who sends others to carry out his orders. But I understand your terms. I would like to see this work." Zeva held her face calm. Her body was jumping with excitement. Finally her patience had paid off! Getting out of her cell was the first step to freedom. She would never embrace the human lifestyle but she had to make them trust her, or at least trust the fact that she was beaten. Then her jailers would grow lax and she could plan her escape.

*  *  *  *  *

## Alcandar

Ravid knew he was close because his nose caught the scent of fresh blood. He didn't bother to check the communication unit secured to his wrist. Four inches wide, the golden bracelet was a mark of his profession. Keenan wore an identical one as he moved beside him. The other team helping them search hadn't reported in but Ravid sniffed the air once more and moved towards the metallic scent.

Each of the four clans that his Judgment Hall was responsible for had female-only grounds. Mature warriors were forbidden to cross onto those areas. Among a race that produced too few females, there was strict law governing their contact with warriors.

But not all warriors agreed on that point.

Tampering with their genetic code had sent the Alcandian race into a new era of struggle. It might be thought that conquering disease meant nothing but happiness. Instead, science had unlocked a whole new chain of threats to life as Alcandians knew it.

Males grew larger and their bodies became more dominant. That had been one of the major mistakes of the Alcandian genetic tampering. Males craved strength. Once it was tapped into, there were parts of the brain that refused to stop at just growth. Buried deep inside their brains were seeds of primitive hunters that grew right along with their bodies. Aggression bloomed with their height.

The need to hunt for a mate went hand in hand with that building of physical strength.

Alcandians were stretched between the ability to manipulate nature itself and the reality that they never should have tampered with life. As the male genes were genetically altered to be stronger and more powerful, they took over the reproductive centers of the brain causing the next generation to be born with dominant numbers of male chromosomes in the sperm.

And that led teams like him and Keenan to a run-down manor house on the outskirts of Bendark territory. Alcandian warriors could psychically link with a female, but only their mate. There was no known formula for finding that rare female. After touching her mind, warriors lost the urge to mate with any female but theirs.

Before that, the enhanced male genes included a need to mate that was fueled by primitive cells that could not be separated from the more civilized ones.

Ravid battled against that demon every day that he and Keenan patrolled their grounds. He believed in the laws that protected females. He wasn't willing to see his homeworld dissolve into a civilization where males preyed on females and used their greater strength to force them into submission.

Keenan stopped as the metallic smell of blood increased. His eyes moved over the tile floor as Ravid stopped in the doorway. They moved in unison because their minds were linked. It made them stronger—harder to defeat. Their thoughts flowed between them as Keenan brushed a doorway curtain aside.

"We are Judgment officials." Keenan kept his voice low as he lowered his body to look at their victim. Her eyes were wide with terror as her feet tried to push her back despite the stone wall her back was against. She was huddled in a ball as Ravid looked at the harsh evidence of Alcandian males who hadn't developed discipline to control their own bodies.

The female was bloody from hard use and her face swollen from abuse. It was a harsh reality that resulted from a male failing to become a warrior. Without honor, a male was a savage who preyed on anything weaker. Whether it was food or mating, the only thing a dishonorable male craved was feeding his own selfish desires.

Ravid raised his arm to contact the other teams searching the area. A memory official would view the female's ordeal through her eyes and hopefully gain enough information to begin tracking the deviants responsible.

"Chandler, we have recovered the female."

There was no reply. Keenan turned his eyes away from the female to look at Ravid. He stood up and attempted contact on his own communication link. Silence made Keenan move through a doorway as Ravid punched in their location before moving along with his companion.

Reaching up, Ravid gave the door curtain a sharp tug to free the fabric from its rod. He reached for their recovered victim and wrapped the length of dirty fabric around her body. Whimpers escaped from her lips despite the fist she had shoved in her mouth. Her eyes flew to his uniform as she tried to break out of terror's hold.

Ravid took her with him into the next room. He was caught between the need to back Keenan up, and protect their victim. Tension filled the air as silence stretched out. Chandler would have answered if the warrior could, the fact that he did not made Ravid move silently through the next room and onto the one connected to it.

There was no blood this time. Death had been delivered to the team of Judgment officials from behind. Their skulls caved in by a heavy blow to each. Rage filled him as Ravid knelt next to Chandler and turned the warrior over. His eyes stared up without seeing as Keenan's anger joined with Ravid's. Judgment officials were family but Chandler was his own blood. The rage inside him boiled until it transfused into his brain on a cellular level. It went beyond emotion. It became a driving need that would haunt both Keenan and himself until blood satisfied it.

* * * * *

## One year later on Earth

It was mindless work, unless you were using it to teach yourself a foreign language. Zeva forced herself to understand the list on her clipboard. She spoke English but had never learned to read it. Her new job was full of little opportunities to learn. Knowledge was the key to her freedom. She watched the warehouse for any and all details that might help in her quest for freedom.

She couldn't give up. Despair stalked her but she resisted its lure. It had been a full year now since the humans had destroyed the wormhole that connected Alcandar to Earth. Just who was right or wrong she wasn't sure about anymore. The only thing that burned clearly was the need to escape.

Her people had built the gate to find mates. Earth was currently evolving into a female species. Alcandians knew that because their race was a millennium older and they had been enduring the same genetic difficulties, only on Alcandar, they were becoming all male. Females on Alcandar were rare. Only one in twenty births was a little girl. The males had turned to the stars to find mates to fill that gap.

Alcandians held the science to prove what humans were only beginning to notice on Earth. The rise in female births was deeply coded into their DNA and increased its effect on their race each generation. Alcandar was willing to share the data in return for allowing their warriors to silently search among the population for mates. Alcandian warriors needed to be able to psychically bridge with a female before they could claim her. It was a matter of honor to the men from her world.

Earth had too many females and while it might be accepted that it was a match made to perfection, humans had resented it. Zeva wasn't sure anymore. Alcandian warriors claimed their mates when and where they found them. It was based on their abilities to mind-bridge. Once that happened, the female was taken back to Alcandar. It was easy to see how humans might view that as plundering.

What humans didn't see was the tradition that surrounded those introduction rituals. Females, even ones taken from other races, were never allowed to be hurt. Warrior could tempt and attempt to corner them into passion but force was not tolerated beyond taking the female to Alcandar.

Zeva looked at the open warehouse door and sighed. She did understand how that could be considered barbaric. Alcandian warriors had more determination than any creature she had ever encountered. They were relentless when they believed they had found their mate.

Two faces floated through her memory. Keenan and Ravid. They were two Alcandian warriors who had been stalking her before her abduction. The two men were sculpted to perfection and she shivered at just their memory, but the idea of allowing them too near her sparked a fear deep inside her heart. Her temper often flared up as she thought about that cowardice. She did not like finding it inside herself.

Alcandian warriors trained for battle every day. They grew far taller than humans, and even at her height of six feet, her head didn't reach Ravid's shoulder. In his embrace she would be helpless. Shame tugged at her because Ravid was a warrior. The man had honor and would never harm a female, but still the fear showed up every time she felt one of the two men near her.

A little smile tugged her lips up. Yes, both men circled her. The humans held that little Alcandian fact against her race as well. When an Alcandian male was in his youth he always chose a companion. It was another male he could trust with his very life. If he ever went into battle, the two fought as one, a kind of team that made them even more fierce and harder to defeat. They mind-bridged to make it possible to communicate and thereby bonded into a form of brotherhood that was sometimes even stronger than death.

Keenan was Ravid's companion and the two were feared on parts of Alcandar. They were Judgment officials, enforcers of the law on other warriors. The two warriors didn't negotiate or listen to pleas, they imposed their duty with iron strength.

A shiver raised goose bumps on her bare forearm. Zeva looked at the reaction and frowned. She had never let either man get close enough to touch her mind but they had been crowding her into a smaller circle every day before she was captured. Warriors were not allowed in the unbound female areas of Alcandar.

Once a warrior found his mate, a fever ignited inside him. If the female was too young for binding it might drive the male insane while he waited for her to grow up. Zeva rubbed her arms to smooth out the bumps. Whatever reaction she might have to Ravid did not matter now. The man was an entire planet away and so was Keenan.

It was both warriors who wanted her. Alcandian unions were not monogamous. This time her thoughts made her smile as a pair of human military men walked by. The humans acted disgusted by her homeworld customs but three-member mating groups were very practical on a world where there were too few females. Some warriors even had two companions and therefore they would have only one female among the three males. When one member of a warrior union became interested in a female, his brother-at-arms immediately shared his thoughts. They either shared her or fought over her.

And that had left her struggling to outsmart both Ravid and Keenan. It had not been simple and Zeva still battled with the fear that drove her to do it. Not that it mattered here in her prison, but alone with her thoughts, the two men's faces refused to leave her in peace. It felt like they were reaching for her across the expanse of space.

Maybe they were. Zeva didn't know for sure. She was to blame for that. She had kept to the female areas of her home despite the fact that she had reached her *Triparh*. Her Alcandian maturity birthday. At twenty-four she was allowed and encouraged to mingle with the male population until she encountered a warrior who could touch her mind.

Her thoughts went somber as she thought about her mother leading her out of the female section that first time. Paneil was so proud of her daughter! Zeva had followed her mother because she just didn't have the heart to disappoint her. It had been a secret relief to pass that first day without feeling the burning sensation of contact in her head.

As that first day had been joined by others and turned into weeks and seasons, Zeva had relaxed back into her own life. She had her own studio where she trained girls in the Alcandian art of self-defense. Truthfully, she was relieved to be able to return to her life without the complication of binding mates. Binding with any warriors meant submission and that was something that her soul rebelled against. There was something wrong with her. Alcandian girls looked forward to mind-bridging with their mates, yet Zeva wanted to avoid it like death. The idea of being pressed between the hard bodies of warriors struck her as helpless and it turned her blood as cold as ice.

So she had found reason to not mingle with males. Her mother had voiced objections but there was a comfort inside her studio that grew more enticing every day that Zeva didn't let Paneil drag her out of it.

Ravid and Keenan had walked right into her studio. Judgment officials were the only warriors who traveled over the gender boundaries without penalty. The two huge males had silently appeared in the doorway and searched out their prey. It had been a move of ruthless precision that she remembered in detail. The way they moved was deadly. Their eyes slashed through you in seconds, baring your deepest thoughts to their precise mental interrogations.

Judgment officials used their psychic abilities to search for truth in their investigations. Teams like Ravid and Keenan held absolute authority when they were hunting. Both warriors wore dark maroon coats that signified their enforcement status. The black binding of those long coats told her they were also empowered to impose death if necessary.

Warriors like that were rare even in the male sections. They kept to themselves and only socialized with other Judgment officials. Zeva didn't even know where they lived, except that it was on Judgment grounds. Information was kept completely confidential on warriors like them. It was meant to shield their families from retribution but Zeva couldn't help thinking that it suited the two warriors.

Ravid had stepped into the front doorway at exactly the same moment Keenan entered the back door. It was silent but lethal in its execution. One moment her studio was full of training girls and the next everybody was shocked into frozen horror as the two pairs of eyes moved over each and every face. Zeva felt her frustration rise as the memory played its way through her mind. Both warriors had scanned her studio and settled on one girl. A nineteen-year-old who had only begun classes with her shortly before that day. One touch from Ravid's mind and the girl had panicked. Zeva had no idea why she interfered, but it was her studio and impulse sent her across the floor despite the fact that she knew the two warriors held the authority to do whatever they wanted with the girl.

Both warriors closed the distance to their target on swift strides. Her other students had parted, frantic to avoid any contact with them. Like a frightened herd of mares, they had scurried aside as the predators targeted one of their number and they gratefully gave them free passage as long as it would satisfy them and gain the rest of the herd freedom.

Zeva had been furious. Her student was terrified and she didn't care what the reason was, only that warriors didn't have the right terrorize her students! She moved into Ravid's path and still smiled over the astonished expression that crossed his eyes as she stood between him and his prey. She'd tipped her head back and glared at the warrior.

"You are disrupting my class and there are no shoes permitted on the mat."

A corner of Ravid's mouth had twitched with amusement before he clamped his lips into a solid line. His eyes moved over her face before he stepped closer and loomed over her. His eyes flashed with a current of blue as her body went hot. The wave of heat had been so intense, she'd almost folded at the knees. A frown appeared on his mouth as his huge hands curled around her biceps. Just a whisper of a touch before the student let out a scream behind her.

Ravid lifted her out of his path as he went to help Keenan. Her student aimed her hardest blows at the man as she tried to escape. Keenan looked annoyed as he turned to block the attacks with non-vital parts of his body. He raised his topaz eyes to his partner as Ravid dropped her and captured the student in arms that encircled the girl completely. "Be still."

The command had been full of arrogant strength but not ego. Both warriors could back up that arrogance. It was more than strength of body, it poured from them like water. Everything else was swept up in the rushing current. Even with his arms full, Ravid had shot Keenan a look that caused the warrior to look at her with curiosity. Every nerve ending on her skin had snapped with a rush of emotion. Zeva felt her stomach twist with just the memory. Two more maroon-clad warriors appeared in the doorway to break the odd contact.

Her body refused to forget that pulse of energy. Zeva labeled it anger over her studio being invaded but there was a nagging doubt that tugged on her thoughts. Little details of both men were floating around her brain, the way their coats spread over wide chests, the powerful legs that she'd viewed as they moved across her studio floor. Everything shouted out their incredible strength and her body quivered with that knowledge.

She did not understand her reaction to them. Everything she had ever trained for all boiled down to control — discipline was only another name for control. Ravid and Keenan dissolved the very foundation of who she defined herself to be.

Instead she was stuck on Earth. Zeva slammed a stack of splotch-painted fabric onto a shelf and stood up. The warehouse was perfect for her quest to understand the English words on her list.

A smile curved her lips. She did understand and very soon she was going to free herself. Where was she going? Who cared! Any free life would be better than captivity. She would blend into the human population with a little practice.

* * * * *

*Alcandar*

"I will enforce justice." Ravid wasn't sure who he was trying to convince with his words. His brother's widow looked at him before she nodded her head. Keenan's hand landed on his shoulder as Amin stood up and walked across the hall. Ravid looked at Keenan with a dark frown. "We almost had them today."

Keenan only raised an eyebrow. Almost wasn't nearly good enough. Helmut and Craddock were deviants of the worst kind. They killed like animals and preyed on their own

18

females. The trail wasn't cold but it was a hunt that had consumed them both for an entire year now. The only good thing Keenan could think about the last year was the fact that they did not have a mate to worry about protecting while they pressured the deviants.

Zeva's image floated through his head and Keenan couldn't stop it from snagging his interest. Details from their brief meetings were etched into his memory. It left him hungry for more information about her. Things like the sound of her voice when she was happy and the scent of her skin. Deeper cravings lingered in his head as he considered what her lips tasted like.

Ravid growled as the image floated into his head. Keenan watched his companion's eyes brighten. Leaving his drink on the table, Keenan stood up. "I wish to check the progress on the gate."

Ravid stood as well and the two left the eating hall. With their hunt for Helmut and Craddock stalled for the moment, they turned to the next order of business. Retrieving Zeva from Earth. They would be the first warriors allowed through the new gate being constructed between Alcandar and Earth.

Retrieving their citizen was the first order of business, and Ravid and Keenan held the assignment because they were the only Judgment officials who had ever encountered her. As brief as those contacts had been it could grant them the advantage in finding her.

Ravid curled his lips back from his teeth and growled. It was one assignment he was going to enjoy…completely.

"As will I." Keenan's voice was low and hard as he cast a side-glance at Ravid. His body was tight with need that shot through his blood and even into his cock. It was the beginning of a mind-bridging. The proof that could not be denied, Zeva was their mate. On Earth, Zeva wouldn't hide behind a border and Keenan found himself enjoying the fact that he wouldn't be bound by Alcandian law while he searched for her.

\* \* \* \* \*

## Six weeks later on Alcandar

"This gate is viable." A mutter of approval rippled over the room as a grey-haired warrior studied his computer data. In the background, there was the electronic hum of a newly engaged gate. It was a wormhole built to be used as a portal. The opposite end of this one was on Earth in a remote part of the Sierra Nevada forest. Despite the humans' knowledge of their technology, they did not have the ability to detect a new gate. While the new gate was almost identical to its predecessor, their frequency was different and the humans did not know that the portal could be constructed with different light speed signatures.

Even if they could decode the signal, the gate would have been built. The blue current of light offered survival to Alcandar. Without females from other races their own would continue its decline into a solely male race. Fresh DNA was essential to rebuilding a healthy society and Earth had a perfect match in their evolution towards the female gender.

Honor had demanded they attempt to negotiate with the planet's government. Having failed, they would turn to taking what they needed. Earth had too many females and it was only fair that humans learned to share. It was a battle for survival and not a single Alcandian warrior was willing to walk away from it.

The gate portal began to fill with the first wave of warriors willing to risk their lives to search for a mate. Their faces were alight with eagerness to begin and not a single one looked back. A pair of Judgment officials moved forward and the warriors parted for this elite pair. They wore human clothing and had large backpacks on their backs. The portal ended deep in a cavern in the heart of a glacier-carved granite valley. Once on the planet, they would have to hike out of the forest before entering the populated areas that might yield females.

Keenan eyed his companion and grinned as the gate filled the room with its blue light. "I agree with you, Ravid."

"On what?"

"That this is a duty I enjoy far more than I should."

Ravid stepped closer to the portal. "A warrior must take his comforts where he can, Keenan." Ravid laughed before he stepped into the gate. Enjoyment had been missing from his life for too long. But finding Zeva wasn't filling him with elation. Icy cold fear rose from the idea that he might bring her back. The craving to touch her remained and touching her could awaken far more than just a craving.

Binding fever was more powerful than any warrior's discipline. If Zeva was his mate she would also become the only soft spot that deviants like Helmut and Craddock could use to strike at him and Keenan.

Remaining unbound seemed far more intelligent.

# Chapter Two

## ဆා

Cole Somerton smiled before his chest rumbled with amusement. Oh sweet! The day was here at last. There was a reason a man needed to listen to that little gut-twisting instinct that warned him not to trust someone too far. Keeping a little insurance was always a good idea no matter who you were dealing with.

His face went serious as he looked at the little bit of Alcandian technology he'd secreted away over two years ago. This one thing that he had failed to report to his commanding officer. Well, maybe it wasn't such a little thing. Just a key to tracking any further wormhole activity on Earth's surface. The Alcandian portals had to operate in a single bandwidth of frequency, but contained in that band were forty-two different sub-dimensions that might be used. Sure, he'd reported the bandwidth but forgotten to mention the sub-dimensions. It was sort of like pointing out the yard line in a football game but not showing your fans that yards were made up of inches.

Maybe he'd always suspected Rinehart would knife him in the back. Rage boiled slowly through his bloodstream. Cole sort of enjoyed the burn of anger, it had been his companion for a solid year now. Every damn friend he thought he had was a goddamn liar. Men he would have gone to war with turned out to be bigots. They called themselves "human purists" and condemned him as an "alien-lover".

He chuckled even lower as he caught sight of his frame in the bathroom mirror. Alcandar was an interesting place. There were all sort of interesting side effects to living on the planet. Ingesting their genetically advanced food had unlocked his pituitary gland and set off another growth spurt just like a teenager. His frame had widened and his bones thickened and now he towered over men he'd once looked in the eye.

The mirror showed him a seven-and-half-foot giant who resembled an Alcandian warrior more than a human. Cole grinned. He picked up the flashing, portable scan detector and stared at the Alcandian symbols flashing on the screen. His grasp of the language wasn't strong enough to translate it but he knew exactly where to find a good translator.

Zeva would be relieved to hear that Alcandar was once again joined to Earth with a wormhole portal. Cole grabbed a duffel bag and tossed in a few necessities. He looked around the spartan quarters that York had banished him to and sneered. He wasn't coming back either. He knew where Zeva was, and with her help they would leave Earth far behind. York and Rinehart were welcome to their human pride.

But they were not welcome to imprison Zeva in some twisted plot to bend Alcandar to their will. Call him a traitor, Cole intended to see to her return to her home personally.

Or die trying.

* * * * *

"Zeva, don't you think it's time to call it a night?"

No, she didn't, but Zeva couldn't let Cassandra know that. Night was just falling. Winter season brought sunset far earlier than summer and Zeva had been counting the days until the Earth moved away from its main star. She needed the cover of darkness to escape. "I just want to finish this last page."

"Why?" Cassandra leaned against the doorframe and gave Zeva a bored look. "There will just be another list tomorrow."

That was true enough but Zeva aimed a small smile at the human girl to soothe her. She really did harbor some affection for the human. Cassandra was a likable girl but that did not change Zeva's determination to flee. "I just enjoy finishing what I begin."

Cassandra shook her head and stood up. "You're a better woman than I, Zeva. Whatever turns you on." She turned and went back into the office that housed the warehouse paperwork and computer system.

Smiling with triumph, Zeva lowered her arm. All the blood had flowed down the limb because she'd held it up against the metal shelving. Reaching for a small bar of soap she'd hidden among the boots, she smeared it over her hand and wrist. A black location beacon was strapped to her wrist. The thing replaced her prison walls by transmitting her location to her jailers. For three weeks she had starved herself to lose enough weight to slip the thing off.

With the help of the soap, the black binding slipped over her hand and off. Zeva nodded with satisfaction as she held her captivity in the palm of her hand. Her smile faded as she looked at the office. She had to take care of Cassandra. Distaste rose in her throat but Zeva tightened her resolve. The girl wouldn't leave without escorting Zeva back to her secured housing and she would raise an alarm out of duty if she found Zeva missing.

Zeva needed time to get off the base. Moving towards the office, Zeva struck silently. Cassandra's blonde head fell to her desk with only a slight thud as a blow to her head thrust her into unconsciousness.

"Couldn't have done it better myself."

Zeva hissed with rage and turned to face her company. She tightened her fingers into fists as she steeled herself to deal another blow. She would not fail tonight!

"Hello Zeva."

Recognition flashed across Zeva's eyes as she noticed the black location bracelet dangling from one of Cole's fingers. He smirked at her as he held it up. "Very nice work. What's the rest of your plan?"

Zeva felt her heart leap. Confidence surged through her as she drank in the details of Cole's face. It had been far too long since she had looked on the face of a friend! He was the only human she would have been happy to see and her face couldn't contain her joy. "I have a bag hidden with clothing. A hat and the same uniform your soldiers wear."

Cole nodded approval. "And the security gate?" Her blank look made him cuss. His eyes moved over the office looking for anything to use for their escape. "Get dressed now."

Zeva didn't hesitate. She had managed to pry open a small window and it wouldn't be very long before someone reported that she had not arrived back at her housing. The sound of the faucet running filled the office right before she finished.

Cole had handcuffed Cassandra and had the girl's head leaning against his chest while he stood behind her. Looking up he nodded approval at her clothing and lifted a coffee cup of water. "We need an hour or we don't stand a chance. They'll run us down on the road with a helicopter."

Cole turned the mug over and dumped the water on Cassandra's face. She jerked and muttered as she came around. Cole's fingers clamped over her mouth as her eyes focused and her body jerked. He held her in a sturdy grip as she yelled through his hand.

"Listen very carefully, Sergeant. If you want to live you are going to do exactly what I tell you to." His words were ice-cold. Zeva blinked her eyes because she wasn't sure it was the same man she remembered as a friend. Cole's eyes were razor-sharp as he lifted the phone and transferred his hand to Cassandra's hair. "We just want to leave. Tell the housing staff you're working late. Mess up and you'll be dead before they punch the alarm."

His face was absolutely ruthless. Zeva forced her eyes to be just as sinister. Cassandra trembled as her blue eyes fluttered between them both and Cole tightened his grip on her hair. "Just do it, Sergeant. Tell them you need an hour, I don't want to break your neck." Her eyes went large with horror as Zeva struggled with her distaste. She couldn't stop Cole—if she did, she condemned herself.

"What's the number? And don't mess up, darling."

Cassandra swallowed and spat out a number. Cole punched it into the phone before holding the receiver to her ear. His hand tugged on the strands of her hair in warning as she took a shaky breath.

"Sergeant Blane, we are finishing a late request." Cassandra's eyes shot a venomous look at Zeva before she drew a deep breath into her lungs. "Yes, I will escort her when we finish. One hour."

Cole dropped the phone and smoothed a hand over Cassandra's head. The girl violently shook her head and glared at him. "Happy?"

"Unfortunately, not yet."

The night air smelled amazing! Zeva felt it slap her cheeks and smiled. The miles fell behind them as Cole punched the accelerator on their jeep. They couldn't keep the motorized transportation very long but it would give them distance.

Cole shot her a heavy look as he controlled his need to go faster. "I'm sorry about Cassandra. It was the only way."

"I understand." Zeva did too. Cole had fished the sergeant's base identification card out of her shirt pocket and used it to get Zeva off the base. In the dark and wearing a winter skull cap, the guards hadn't looked too closely, only noted that she had it.

Zeva consoled her conscience with the knowledge that Cassandra would have done the same thing if she had been the prisoner. Their time together had formed a fragile relationship that Zeva would consider her only fond memory of Earth. The human might not be her friend because of her orders to be her warden, yet Cassandra had not been unkind in the execution of her orders.

"Time to trade the jeep in." Cole pulled off the road and pressed a button on his belt. Two doors on an old barn opened and he drove right into the dark interior. A slight motion at her side and the doors closed behind them sealing them in darkness.

"Sorry, no lights. I don't want the neighbors to notice."

A small yellow glow surrounded them and Zeva saw it was a small flashlight. Cole handed it to her as he jumped from the jeep. There was a car of some kind next to them.

"There're clothes on the front seat, Earth female civilian clothing. Put it on and get in."

Zeva reached for the door handle and heard Cole do the same on the driver's side. He yanked his splotch-colored shirt over his head and reached into the car for a blue shirt.

"Thank you, Cole. You are a man of honor."

He grinned over the roof of the car. "We make a good team. I had no idea how we were going to get that location beacon off you."

And she had not known about the security gate. Zeva pulled the odd clothing from the seat and began to change. She was delighted to get rid of the splotch-painted clothing because it represented her captivity. If she never saw it again she would be grateful!

Cole moved around the back of the car and opened the trunk of it. "Toss me your clothes." Zeva did it and watched him take his changed clothing and hers and lay it in the trunk bed. He frowned before aiming his eyes around the dimly lit garage. He moved on determined steps and stripped a cover off some kind of large farming machine. He shook the bulky piece of fabric and dust flew off it. He grunted before returning to the open trunk and stuffing the fabric into it. Understanding dawned as Zeva watched the careful attention Cole gave to the task.

27

"We are taking her with us?"

"Have too." Cole finished his work and stood up. "I bought this car with cash. The registration hasn't been changed yet and the owner is on a cruise ship somewhere in the Caribbean. There is nothing to link us to it except Cassandra. If they find this barn and her, she'll tell them we changed cars and what to look for. It would be her duty." Cole moved towards the back of the jeep. Actually he could kill her but that wasn't an option in his mind. The sergeant was a complication that he hadn't planned on but he needed her to get Zeva off the base. Now, he just had to keep her under wraps long enough to get Zeva to the mouth of that portal.

Cassandra blinked as the dim light hit her eyes. Cole pulled free the heavy cover he'd hidden her under as she glared at him. Silver duct tape sealed her mouth closed and three pairs of handcuffs secured the sergeant in the footwell in the back of the jeep.

"Sorry, honey, but I couldn't have you sounding off at that checkpoint." Cole lifted her right out of the jeep as she squealed behind the tape. His long legs carried him back to the open trunk as he laid her in it. There was a metallic click of handcuffs as he unhooked her feet from her wrists and laid her out straight.

Zeva turned back around. She couldn't feel sorry for the other woman. Cole handled her with care and that would have to be enough. Cassandra was bound by her duty to raise the alarm and Zeva wouldn't go back to her imprisonment.

The car rocked as the trunk was closed and Cole opened the driver's door. Zeva slipped in beside him and watched him press the door opener.

"Here." A slim Alcandian tracking device was tossed into her lap. Tears pricked her eyes as Zeva held the item from her homeworld. The smooth case made it seem almost more real. Memories had kept her sane for an entire year of solitude. The only pleasant part of that year was locked in the trunk and hating her at the moment, but Zeva looked at the screen and let her hungry eyes soak up her own language.

"You didn't give this to your superiors." It wasn't a question. Zeva looked at Cole and grasped the knowledge that he had really planned to come for her all along. He had just been waiting for the right time.

Cole drove their newest transportation out of the garage and pushed the button on his waist again. He stopped the car and looked at her. "I would have smuggled my own sister off Alcandar if that was what she wanted, Zeva. No woman should be a captive."

He left the car and grabbed a large tree branch lying beside the road. Using his superior size he began to sweep the ground they had driven over, erasing the fresh tire marks. Finished, Cole picked up two large basket containers of dried leaves and dumped them over the driveway. He tossed the two containers behind some shrubs and headed back to the car.

Cole Somerton was a rare human. Zeva felt her lungs fill for the first time in months with a truly deep breath as her shoulders lifted. Lifting the beacon in her hand she read the information being fed to it.

Alcandar.

Home.

She would never belong to anyone again. Ever.


Mind over matter. One slow breath in and one slow release of it. The car tire hit a bump and Cassandra cussed behind her tape gag. Her body bounced and she squeezed her eyes shut before her stomach twisted with nausea again. Thank God she hadn't eaten dinner!

One slow breath...

Oh hell, she was going to kill him! Temper flared across her brain and she didn't even try to control the string of profanity that filled her thoughts. In this case she figured her mother would forgive her.

Cole Somerton, she knew his name all right! That name was whispered in the mess hall and most of the corners of the base. He was the man who wouldn't jump on the alien-hate bandwagon. Every other member of the now disbanded team had loudly denounced the planet and proclaimed how much they had done for Earth...

Everyone except Cole Somerton.

Cassandra might not know anything about the Alcandar project but she did know that Zeva was a person, not some evil force come to destroy Earth.

The car bounced her again and she moaned. Tomorrow she would be covered with bruises, but at least whatever Cole had stuffed around her kept her from splitting her skin open as her bound body was jostled.

Cassandra growled and shut her eyes again. *One breath in and slowly release it...*


"We walk from here."

Zeva looked up from her beacon and at the parking lot Cole turned into. There were a few cars parked and most of them had fabric wrapped around them.

"What is this place?"

Cole turned the car off and pushed his door open. "It's a trailhead. These mountains are covered with backpacking trails. If you say the map leads north then we have to cover the rest of the distance on foot. Stealing a helicopter would have sort of blown my idea for slipping out under their noses."

Zeva stepped into the morning sunshine and smiled. It was silent and so serene you could hear the breeze as it moved through the trees. No walls. Zeva smiled as she turned around in a circle and saw the trees and the clouds and not one damn wall! She would crawl up a mountainside if it meant seeing her home again.

"What about Cassandra?" The need to run towards her own people tore at her but Zeva couldn't leave the Earth girl in danger either. They couldn't turn Cassandra loose if they needed to hike. When she sounded the alarm, the men looking for them could gain access to a helicopter.

"She walks with us." Cole opened the trunk and carefully lifted Cassandra from it. Zeva watched the way he handled the woman but couldn't find any fault with it. Anger blazed through her at the dilemma the humans had put her in. All Zeva craved was to leave but she would have to pull this woman with her or risk losing her freedom.

"A little walk, Sergeant, and you'll be free to go." Cole pulled the tape off Cassandra's face and winced at the sound it made. She didn't yell. Instead her eyes bulged with fury making his lips twitch with the urge to smile. Her blonde hair was tangled around her face and she stood there shooting daggers at him.

Spunk. In a woman it was his fatal weakness. Cole looked at the sprinkle of freckles dusting her nose and frowned. Reality sucked sometimes.

Pressing a bottle of water into her hands, Cole bent to unlock the handcuffs around her ankles. "Relax, Sergeant, we just want to leave. Behave yourself and you can be on your way back down this trail tonight."

Cassandra tipped the water bottle up to hide her expression. She drank slowly from the bottle as she tried to bring her thoughts into line. Fear was trying to plant crazy images of her body lying on the side of a backpacker's trail but Cole's face didn't look like a cold-blooded killer's to her.

Oh great! Now she was trusting her captor! That was a common survival instinct that kidnapping victims succumbed to during hostage ordeals. Cole moved away and she stared at the raw strength of his body. He was huge and packed with thick muscle. It was the sort of thing you saw in barbarian movies but never actually expected to meet face-to-face.

Cassandra shook her head and opened her eyes to find Zeva in front of her. The Alcandian looked at her with large dark eyes and a face that looked different. Cassandra couldn't stop the little giggle that shook her chest. She trapped it in her mouth but Zeva's eyes sparkled slightly.

Cassandra shrugged. "I guess I'd be mighty glad to go home too."

"I didn't want to hurt you, Cassandra. But I cannot stay here."

Cassandra tossed her head and twisted the cap back onto the water bottle. "You didn't hurt me."

Zeva grinned and angled her head to look at the side of Cassandra's face. "That bruise says otherwise."

"Barely notice it." Which was true. Cassandra's dad would have been proud of the offhand comment. She hadn't seen her face, so truly, she really hadn't investigated what she looked like. The way she felt said she'd be a black and blue mess tomorrow but she could just save that unveiling for a time when she was all done with the current business of being abducted.

"Let's go." Cole rounded the car and tossed a bottle of water to Zeva. His blue eyes targeted her and Cassandra began walking. She was already trusting the brute, there was no reason to give him an excuse to touch her again. Her soft brain had noticed just how tender his hands could be on her and she really, really, really did not need to go there!

\* \* \* \* \*

Ravid listened to the night and growled. He could smell human on the night breeze. His senses caught each little sound because he was immersed in them. Hunting brought out the basic instincts in a male and he enjoyed the harsh rush of tension. He was balanced on the edge with his companion helping to counterbalance him. Keenan was close by watching the night just as he was.

Mission goals floated through his head but Ravid was enjoying the surge of victory. It had been too long since he and Keenan had bested the odds.

*Zeva.*

Need rose from her name as he looked at the face in his memory. He had touched her so briefly but the moment was burned into his soul. Learning facts about mind-bridging didn't prepare a warrior to recognize it when it happened. All Ravid knew was that something drew him to Zeva and their separation was eating him alive.

A female willing to stand in the path of Judgment officials was rare. It spoke of a level of confidence that frankly astonished Ravid. He wanted to search her eyes for the spark of defiance he remembered her flinging at him before duty pulled him away from her. He had just barely brushed her mind and that half moment of contact burned incessantly for him to renew the contact.

Caution tried to banish that craving but it was losing its hold on the need flowing from the slight touch of mind to mind. Ravid could feel Zeva, she was getting closer and that information shut his logic down. Instinct refused to let him consider the consequences.

Moving forward, Ravid felt Keenan on his heels. Their minds were fused together as they surged forward on their hunt.

* * * * *

Zeva froze in her tracks. Her heart suddenly accelerated and her lungs frantically increased their pace to keep up. Her body shivered as fear strangled her. Her eyes went large as she frantically looked around her.

Coming.

They were coming. Her skull felt like it was being ripped open and exposed. Solid walls pressed in on her from the force bearing down on her. Control slipped through her fingers like sand, leaving her body falling as it poured down and took her with the stream.

Ravid materialized from the night like a demon from her worst nightmare. Zeva could smell his skin as his eyes targeted hers and he burst inside her head. She spun in a crazy circle to find Keenan. She knew he would be there too. Instinct demanded she keep them both in sight as her heart beat at a frantic pace, propelling her blood through her veins too fast for her lungs to keep oxygenated.

"Get out!" Her voice was an agonized demand as her vision blurred. Everything pressed in on her as Keenan's eyes cut into hers. He surfaced inside her head with Ravid and the tension exploded. Her lungs froze as her heart pounded faster and Keenan's eyes were the only thing she saw as the weight of both warriors crashed in on her. Her head was too full of them to endure and she launched her body away from the suffocating weight of the two warriors.

But she couldn't escape herself. Her blood surged forward as she actually caught their scent. She was cruelly stretched between elation at seeing her own race and despair that the two warriors were ones who could reach into her thoughts.

Ravid's eye's glowed with primal instinct and there was a part of her that smiled in response. Confusion hit her in a wave. It tore at her with fear and need all mixing together to taunt her with imperfect solutions.

Leaving Earth meant dealing with Ravid and Keenan. Staying condemned her to an existence of being an outcast.

Ravid spat out a curse under his breath. The sign of his temper made him more real in that moment. Zeva shifted on her feet and raised an open hand at him. "Stay out of my mind."

Her rejection cut him deeply. Ravid wanted to jerk her back next to his body and teach her to enjoy his touch. Her heart fluttered at an alarming rate as she battled to overcome her own attraction.

"I think we have tried." Keenan's voice was low and soft but Ravid felt the burn of the other warrior's rage. He considered Zeva with a dark frown before he leaned forward and sniffed the air. "Yet it is proven."

Zeva clamped her control in place as she closed her arms around her body to hide the little tremors still shaking her limbs. It was just shock from so many days yearning for this moment. Once she was home her body would stop acting so foolishly. She forced herself to believe that. She looked away because her body wanted to bask in the glow of what she witnessed in the two warriors' eyes. Temptation taunted her with the idea that they found her attractive. "I would like to go home."

"Then we agree." Keenan watched the flare of rejection cross Zeva's face. Caution broke through his flaring senses long enough for him to remember that they were not alone. "Yet we will discuss this later."

Zeva's eyes flew back to his and the contact was undeniable. It burned from his mind into Ravid's mind as Zeva filled both their thoughts. She was drawn to them just as strongly as they sought her.

"Aye, we shall." And she would end it...somehow. Zeva felt the emotion seep into her body even as she tried to get it to just flow away. Her flesh turned traitor as it hummed with sensation.

Ravid turned towards the scent of human with a snarl. The lack of a battle left him longing for an outlet for a year of pent-up frustration. The warrior he found facing him brought him up short.

"Hello Ravid." Cole pushed Cassandra towards a large granite boulder and watched her out of the corner of one eye. She leaned against the rock and crossed her arms over her chest. Her eyes were glued to Ravid as the Alcandian flexed his fingers.

Cole enjoyed the brush of psychic sense against his mind. He was more at home with the contact than among humans who shunned the ability. The night yielded other men who came closer as they inspected his thoughts for any excuse to label him a threat.

They were Ravid's fellow Judgment officials, Cole was certain of that fact. Seven men in all. They each looked over Zeva before granting him a harsh nod of their heads.

A year of planning and waiting and this would see the completion of his last mission. Cole didn't regret his choice...only that York had forced him into making one. "Good bye, Zeva, I hope your luck is better on Alcandar."

"That won't take much of an improvement." But she really couldn't keep the remorse out of her head. She would miss Cole and the man had destroyed what remained of his own life by helping her. There were too many cameras on that base and although the humans that manned them had not discovered Cole's deception in time to stop them, they no doubt would be waiting for Cole with their idea of justice for traitors.

Cole turned to see to the last detail of his plan but Ravid stepped into his path. "How did you find us?"

Cole grinned at the warrior and pointed at Zeva. "Zeva's got a little tracking device that doesn't belong on Earth, my friends. Take it home with you before someone shows up to ruin our little happy ending."

One of Ravid's fellow officials reached into Zeva's pocket and withdrew the tracking unit. He raised an eyebrow at Ravid before dropping the unit to the ground and smashing it with a boot heel. He scooped up the destroyed device and tucked it into his pocket. "You have honor, human. I am surprised." He pointed at Cassandra and moved closer. He stared at her wide eyes intently before shaking his head. "I cannot bridge with her but we should take her with us."

"No." Cole stepped in front of Cassandra to stare at the warrior. "I didn't free one woman just to place another one in her place." Cole turned to look at Ravid. "Take Zeva home and complete your mission. I'll finish mine out by getting Cassandra out of this wilderness."

"I will accompany you, Cole Somerton." Eyes shifted as one of the warriors moved forward. His eyes considered Cassandra before she frowned and bit into her lower lip. The warrior looked back at Cole. "I am Dyne. I will erase the memory from her mind. This gate must remain secret."

"Oh great." Cassandra rolled her eyes and shot Cole's warning look right back at him. "Save it for someone who's impressed, Somerton. But hey, if you are talking about making me forget about being stuffed in a truck for hours on end…who am I to argue?"

"We could just take you with us." Dyne sounded amused by the idea.

Cassandra shrugged and faked a yawn. "So I heard, but you know, I really don't need to be walked home. I can get there all by myself."

"It would be simpler to take you with us, yet it would be dishonorable."

Cassandra fluttered her eyelashes and Zeva stifled her laughter. Warriors took everything way too serious. Dyne was a memory shifter. The Judgment official would move the memory to a part of her subconscious where it would not surface. It was a calm ending to a year that had felt endless.

Her memory reminded her of just where the new gate was and Zeva turned towards it. She ached to get her feet off this wretched planet and back onto her home. Cassandra did not need her and she just couldn't wait any longer.

Her legs moved her over the uneven ground with amazing speed. Zeva moved faster as she felt Ravid behind her. She didn't respond to her name being called, instead she ducked into the mouth of a dark cavern and walked right into the heart of the blackness.

Tiny fingers of blue light reached through the thick darkness. Zeva lifted her hands towards the signs of home. The air was chilled but her heart beat quickly and her blood warmed her cold skin. Her feet closed the distance to the blue glow until she reached the room where the gate formed.

A hundred feet of pulsing blue current split the cavern. Blackness surrounded it as it twisted and hummed. Zeva didn't stop, she was drawn to it, to the promise of her own life.

Freedom screamed at her as she felt Ravid and Keenan closing the distance behind her. She jumped towards the gate as her name erupted like a roar from their wide chests.

"Zeva!" Their voices merged into a single thrust of male threat. Zeva dived into the current as two strong arms caught her body. The pulsing current swept them along with its flow as she was pressed between two hard bodies.

Zeva hated her own body in that moment. She was the weaker being, strength surrounded her taking the form of hard muscles that her own limbs melted against. Her breasts gently lifted as her belly gave a faint twist of need for closer contact with such prime males.

A second later she stood on Alcandar. She shrugged against the embrace but was caught up closer to Keenan who faced her. Ravid took one step and pressed her against his comrade in arms and firmly used his body to trap her there.

"Let me go."

The arms around her tightened for a moment and then granted her request. The fact that she knew it was a request they did not have to grant made her angry. She stared into Ravid's face and bit her lip. "I do not need an escort."

The second they released her, Zeva could breathe again. Her body instantly returned to a measure of control that held some dignity. Maybe it was the fact that she had found the strength to deny what she craved... Zeva didn't know or care. All that mattered was the fact that Keenan and Ravid had stepped away from her.

Her body shivered and she frowned. Temptation taunted her with a strong wave of memory. Both warriors were solid muscle. Between them her body could become a vessel made for pleasure. Her belly gave a harder twist and she recognized just what the sensation was.

*Need.*

The desire to lift her eyelids and look at Keenan pulled at her incessantly, gaining more force as their separation grew larger. Her head turned without conscious thought as the warrior moved away from her. Zeva couldn't control the need to look at his wide chest just once more. She craved another view of them both even as her feet kept moving away from being contained by their powerful bodies.

Keenan watched her. His eyes targeted her the second she lifted her eyelashes. The moment froze as she felt him. It was a connection that broke through the walls of expectation. Instead they touched on some plane where explanations didn't matter, only sensation did.

One second and Keenan surged forward. She had always thought him the calmer one. Zeva jumped away as his body tightened and sprang towards her. Ravid caught his companion's arm and Keenan's face tightened with anger. Zeva turned away and shook her head.

Stupid foolish emotions!

Warning flashed through her brain as longing twisted her belly. Zeva bit into her lower lip as she lamented both looking and leaving. That didn't make any sense but she was suddenly too tired to care. Fatigue landed on her shoulders so heavy it threatened to crush her beneath its weight. Her brain froze in mid-thought and refused to process information beyond picking up her feet.

# Chapter Three

ഔ

Ravid watched Keenan and grinned. It wasn't a happy expression, instead his lips rose into a taunting little smirk that he enjoyed. Keenan slammed a goblet down and glared at the empty vessel.

For once his companion was the one fighting for control. Ravid took a moment to savor that odd occurrence before his own emotions roiled dangerously. Keenan was not the only one battling the urge to break century-old traditions. Charging into the women's hall tempted him almost beyond the limits of his control.

Zeva was there.

The knowledge moved through his body like fire. So close, he could touch her, discover what her skin felt like, draw her scent into his head and…

Ravid shook his head and grabbed a drink from the center of the table. Keenan growled as it disappeared and punched the command key for another one for himself.

"That will not help." A dark-haired warrior took a seat at the table and kept his face calm. Keenan scowled as Jett, Zeva's brother, let a grin lift his lips. "Truly it will not."

Ravid grumbled but Jett only continued to grin. "Drinking keeps me here." Keenan grunted an approval as he too lifted a goblet.

Jett's face went somber as he nodded his head. "Aye, yet it will do you no good." Jett considered the Judgment Hall and the warriors who sat at nearby tables. He was an Alcandian warrior but a guest in this hall. He was from the Sinlar clan. The Judgment Hall wasn't a place he went to often and there was a large part of him that did not wish to be there tonight. "My mother wishes to thank you for returning Zeva."

"It was our duty." The words sounded flimsy to Keenan even as they came out of his own lips. Jett raised a dark eyebrow at him.

"A pleasant duty for a change, yet we are still thankful."

Both warriors nodded, they were no strangers to being the target of family members' anguish. No mother wished to admit that her offspring would be guilty of lawbreaking.

Ravid drew his hand back before his fingers touched another goblet. His body surged with protectiveness and it balanced his need. Guilt tore at his thoughts as he dropped onto a bench next to Jett. Seeing Zeva's brother here meant she rested under the protection of her family.

*He should leave her there.*

Ravid shot Keenan a look and found his companion struggling against his own desires. Neither of them would win the battle. Zeva was their mate. The contact had triggered a reaction that would only feed on itself until nothing mattered but the raging storm of need.

The only fact that made it bearable was the certain knowledge that Zeva would feel it also. Alcandians were far more advanced than humans. Their brains separated lust from mating fever and Ravid understood the burning sensation sweeping aside his judgment.

It was a binding fever. Soon, nothing would matter but Zeva. But he would not be alone in his need. Keenan shared it through their link and Zeva would awaken to the reality of their union.

That fact gave him no satisfaction. It only fueled his desire to bury his need, suppress it until Helmut and Craddock were dead. Yet even then, he and Keenan were still Judgment officials.

That would never change.

\* \* \* \* \*

Alcandar.

Zeva smelled it before she opened her eyes. She was almost afraid to lift her eyelids and discover it was a manifestation of her desperation. Instead the sound of a *guilatar* floated across her ears and she opened her eyes to see the small yellow bird bathing in a copper urn perched on the windowsill.

The shield was off, letting the morning air flood the room, and Zeva jumped out of the bed to look out at the memory that had kept her sane for a yearlong eternity. The hanging vines were green and covered with white blooms as they twisted down the brown sandstone columns that surrounded the main courtyard outside her sleeping room.

Alcandian women moved across the courtyard in their long jackets and loose pants and there wasn't a single splotch-colored human in sight! Two girls hurried past in a training uniform that her eyes drank in the sight of.

It was her studio colors and Zeva laughed as she watched the two run up the steps and around the corner on their way to class. She twirled around in circles like a little girl with her hands flung out and stopped as she looked at the bathing pool in the room.

Her skin crawled with the need to wash. Zeva tore her Earth clothing away and smiled as she heard the fabric rip. She passed a hand over the controls for the bath and smiled as Alcandian symbols greeted her eyes.

Her world and her language! Such little things that meant so very much when you were denied them!

Zeva splashed into the bathing pool until the water covered her head. The pool was large enough to submerge in if she bent her legs. Her head broke the surface of the water as her smile faded. She looked at the expanse of water and noticed for the first time exactly why Alcandian bathing pools were so big.

They were made for three.

Her nipples tightened despite the warm water covering them and Zeva gasped. Sensation ran from the little hard nubs to her belly where heat began to flicker inside her womb. She dived under the water but the heat remained.

Reaching for soap, Zeva scrubbed at her skin trying to cover the rising sensations. She refused to think about them. Her hair hung in wet hunks down her back and she attacked the thick brown length but groaned as her arms lifted above her head. Her breasts tingled as she moved her arms and it fed the heat moving along her limbs. She was keenly aware of her hard nipples and the slide of water over the soft globes.

Sinking into the water, Zeva rinsed the soap away as the curtain to her chamber swished aside.

"Daughter!"

Paneil hurried into the chamber with two of her friends on her heels. Zeva felt an odd pang of shyness hit her as the women just walked right up to the edge of the pool. It was an unexpected sensation. Alcandian baths were rarely private.

She bent her knees and smiled at her mother. Paneil picked up a pitcher and dipped it into the pool. She dumped it over Zeva's head as Zeva tried to toss aside her reluctance to stand up. Lanai, a golden-haired woman who was considered family, came towards the edge of the pool with a towel.

Zeva bit her lower lip and went towards her. Lanai's son, Dylan, was companion to her brother Jett. When warriors bonded, their families became just as intertwined. Lanai didn't think twice about walking into the bathing chamber and neither did Paneil. Zeva's sudden attack of modesty would be viewed as the oddity.

The towel was wrapped around Zeva's head to hold every strand of her hair out of the pool. Paneil watched with a careful eye as Lanai nodded to her. Her mother pressed a control button and a slight electrical shock passed through the water. Zeva gasped as her heightened nerve endings jerked.

A foul word crossed her mind as she stood up. Pitchers were dipped into the water and poured over her shoulders. The water slid down her skin sending a little ripple of sensation into her womb. Every inch of her flesh wanted to be stroked. Touched and pressed between the hard bodies of…

Grrrrr!

Zeva snapped her teeth together but didn't quite contain her frustration. Her skin doubled its awareness level as every body hair she had was rinsed away with the water. She was smooth and completely bare. It should have made her feel wonderful. Instead she was acutely aware of her bare sex.

That was absurd! Alcandian females never had body hair. Warriors did but women were smooth and free of even a hint of stubble. Zeva hadn't even known how long her pubic hair could grow until she was forced to live in the primitive conditions on Earth. Using a razor to remove the hair was barbaric but better than living with it. She groaned again as she looked down her body at the top of her mons. The skin was smooth and completely bare, the hairs having slid out of their follicles so that there was no stubble left. Ravid would like her this way.

"Zeva? Are you all right?"

Stepping out of the water, Zeva helped pull a towel around her body. The fabric felt rough against her skin and she tucked it tighter against her breasts. Her body could just hurt as far as she was concerned. There would not be any further stimulation that required a certain pair of warriors. Her body could just become used to that fact.

"I am more than all right, Mother. I am home!"

Paneil raised an eyebrow as her eyes scanned Zeva's body with a mother's knowing eye. Zeva tightened her grip on the towel and moved towards the clothing that had materialized on her neat bed.

"I have missed sensible clothing!" The long top garment was a coat that had a high waistline to support her breasts.

There were a pair of pants that were loose and the jacket had open slits up its sides so that her legs were not trapped inside the fabric.

It was so much better than human dresses. Those skirts forced a female to be dependent on either male protection or accept being weaker. Zeva detested their pants almost as much. The seams were too tight and rubbed against her sex.

Alcandian clothing was built for function and practicality. The fabrics were rich and they shimmered with highlights but they were not tucked and folded along a female's curves. That sort of advertisement wasn't necessary in a society where mates were chosen by the ability to merge. Warriors did not follow their erections into binding, instead they followed a full range of senses that settled on a female for so much more than just the coloring of her features or the curve of her bottom.

Her stomach rumbled and the women around her smiled. Dressing didn't take long and they all joyfully walked with her to the women's hall for a meal. Zeva took a last second to toss her ruined Earth clothing into a pile she aimed a designation beam at. Not even a speck of dust remained, and she smiled as the beam turned off. Life would resume and she intended to forget about Earth.

\* \* \* \* \*

Zeva's communications unit chirped for a full minute before she recalled that it was actually someone trying to contact her. She looked at the line of text and stood up. Food lost all appeal as she looked at the summons again. It was from Keenan and she pressed her lips into a tight line before the little surge of excitement broke through and showed up on her face for everyone to see.

Friends and family were clustered around the table. The women's hall was still full as her clan's women ignored their daily work to welcome her home.

"What is it, Daughter?" Paneil stood up and twisted her hands as she took in Zeva's frown. Zeva instantly felt remorse for troubling her mother. The summons was not unexpected, but she hadn't considered that the idea that just seeing Keenan's name would excite her.

"It is nothing to worry about mother. I must go to Judgment Hall today." Several females nodded approval. The ugly realities of crime were often dealt with on Judgment grounds. Zeva did admire Ravid and Keenan their dedication to law. It was warriors like them who allowed life on Alcandar to be something worth longing to return home to.

"Your brother will take you."

Zeva nodded but couldn't help wishing she might go alone. Her brother Jett might see too much. A little sigh escaped her throat. Jett was not her main problem. Ravid and Keenan were. Her ultrasensitive nipples were a huge concern because her body was dissolving into a primitive sea of emotion. The control she'd used to endure her imprisonment was crumbling in the face of yearnings that she had never noticed were hidden in her own brain.

\* \* \* \* \*

"Craddock!" Helmut kicked a pile of debris aside and ran into the lower eating hall of their hideout. It was a rotting pile of rock barely fit for warriors, but they were outlaws, on a world where everything flowed through central computer lines. Any functioning home would transmit their location the second they activated the bathing pool. "Craddock!"

"Outside." Helmut smiled as he moved towards his companion's voice. The scent of smoke hit him as he got closer and his stomach rumbled as he noticed the fresh meat turning over a fire. They were true warriors, not the weak-blooded type who roamed Alcandar now. He and Craddock could survive off the planet and they would never accept the current crap about treating females gently. Strength begat strength. A warrior needed a female who could take his strength to bear his offspring. Alcandian females were too coddled to suit him.

"They brought Zeva back."

Craddock turned away from his kill to look at him. "Did they claim her?"

"Don't know and it does not matter. They chased her before they left." Helmut spat on the ground before kneeling down to look at the cooking meat. "That's good enough for me."

Craddock nodded his head, he didn't care either way. "A cunt will be good." If it wounded Ravid and Keenan while they were at it, so much the better.

\* \* \* \* \*

"I am Greer."

Zeva kept her eyes on the warrior. He was a memory viewer. Alcandian justice was swift because there was no chance of deception. Witnesses were not asked for their recount of events. They were expected to allow a memory viewer to see them firsthand through a psychic link.

A warrior like Greer was extremely rare. Most warriors could only link with their mate and their companion. Greer could link with any Alcandian and in many cases other races.

That was why warriors like Ravid and Keenan wore uniforms edged with black. Zeva looked past Greer to where Ravid and Keenan stood. They were extreme examples of perfection. Her eyes traced the wide shoulders as her belly gave a twist and Zeva looked back at Greer before she lost the meager control she still had.

"I have nothing to hide." Greer gave her a half smile as he reached for the sides of her head. His amusement grew from the fact that she was not accused of any wrongdoing—this was an investigation into Earth's actions. Zeva didn't care for the invasion but she owed it to Cole. His help deserved testament so that he would not be branded an enemy.

Greer entered her thoughts and she shuddered as her mind returned to the moment she had shoved Jessica into the first portal a few seconds before she was dragged away from the link with her homeworld.

Humans had destroyed that gate as she watched, and laughed at her devastation.

\* \* \* \* \*

The walls collapsed in on her.

Zeva struggled to breathe as she was slowly crushed. Not a quick death but one where seconds swelled into eternities that allowed her to wither in agony. She gasped as her heart pounded and her arms strained with every ounce of strength she had to push the restraining straps away from her body so that she could draw breath. A scream of desperation filled her mind as her tormentors clicked another set of bindings over her legs.

*Trapped.*

Death loomed over her as she struggled to fill her lungs and live for just another single moment.

"Zeva."

She surged out of her nightmare and hit a solid wall. Large hands instantly captured hers as she sent her fists at her jailer. Instead of painfully jerking her arms in back of her, Zeva found her body captured in a solid embrace that simply held her instead of restraining her.

"It was a dream, *shihori*." Her eyes popped open as the Alcandian endearment hit her ears. The room was lit with silver starshine and Keenan was a mere shadow. Zeva pushed against his chest even as her fingers took the moment to trace the hard ridge of muscles. His clothing frustrated her because it separated her skin from his.

Her bed shifted as two more hands found her back. Ravid's body heat joined Keenan's as Ravid sent his hands in long strokes down her back. Relief surged through her as her

49

nightmare vanished. Zeva just couldn't hold back the rush of pure delight their touch sent through her.

"I'm fine." Zeva looked around the room as she tried to distract herself from the two warriors.

A male grunt hit her ears as the bed shifted and a large hand cupped her face. Keenan's scent filled her senses as his fingers smoothed over her face. "I would guess you have felt better, yet Greer is just as exhausted if that grants you any satisfaction."

Satisfaction. Her body leapt at that idea as she caught Ravid's scent as well. A wave of need hit her brain and all she longed to do was shut off her thoughts. Right here there was sensation and longing and none of that required her to think — only to feel.

The room brightened a bit and it showed her too much. Her eyes caught the wide chest that she had looked past Greer to admire and this time there was no one to witness her admiration of the two warriors. The room was a small one, most likely a guestroom. A curtain was closed over the doorway and another one covering the wall facing into the center of the building. On Sinlar grounds, that wall would only be a half wall. It was tradition that ensured that females did not need to fear being above stairs with two warriors who surpassed her in strength. Any distress would be heard in the eating hall below. But being above stairs at all was a deviation from Alcandian tradition. She was still a maiden and should be sleeping on female grounds.

The hand cupping her face moved and brought her eyes back to Keenan. Blue electricity flashed across his eyes as her nipples hardened beneath her coat. "This is a witness room. Beyond the curtain is a half wall that overlooks our Judgment eating hall.

Keenan bent his head towards her and inhaled her scent. It triggered a harsh flood of need that burned through his veins. Zeva shivered in response and Ravid smoothed his hands over her arms from behind her. She froze as her body rejoiced. His hands felt amazing on her skin and the flesh hidden under her jacket lamented its confinement.

"I should go home." Zeva shrugged but Ravid only stroked her shoulders again in response. He didn't release her and little tingles moved over her skin like star points. She needed some distance from them before her resolve melted. Zeva gathered her strength and folded her knees under her in order to rise from the bed.

Keenan growled at her. A similar sound hit her back as Ravid pressed closer to her back. The hands moving down her arms stopped being soothing, instead they became confining. Keenan leaned down towards her neck and inhaled again. Her stomach twisted with excitement. But uncertainty shook her spine as she felt their body heat. She was keenly aware of being between their powerful bodies. But that growl echoed in her head because it spoke of an aggression that she had never been the target of before.

"Nay." Keenan's eyes opened and a flash of blue shimmered across them. Zeva shook her head but his arms held her in place. His chest rose as the warrior took a deep breath. That tiny sign of his strained control made her push against his embrace. Her own senses pulled the warm scent of his body into her lungs and she resisted the tremor shaking her belly.

"I will have a taste of you first, *shihori*."

His mouth thrust her denial back into her throat. His kiss was firm but not hard. His lips traced hers before pressing her to open her mouth for him. He gently pressed her lips apart as the tip of his tongue stroked over the sensitive surfaces. A soft moan rose from her throat as Ravid found the column of her neck with his mouth. The contact was too hot as Keenan's kiss remained slow and unhurried. The huge warrior took his time tasting her mouth. The tip of his tongue stroking her tongue as Ravid laid a trail of tiny bites along her neck.

Zeva couldn't decide what to do. Her body pulsed with the need to move but she couldn't figure out where she wanted to go. Her fingers curled into talons that gripped Keenan's coat. Temptation urged her to yank on the fabric until she found the male skin she smelled beneath it. Pride demanded that she use that grip to shove the demanding warrior away from her body before he found the hard tips of her nipples.

"*Shihori.*" Keenan's voice was rocky. Zeva trembled as she listened to the ragged sound from the half of the team that she had always viewed at the calmer male. His large hand had slipped into her hair and cupped the back of her head. The grip didn't hurt but it was solid...just like Keenan. Her logic screamed against the heat flowing into her belly as Ravid caught the side of her head and turned it to accept his kiss.

Hard and determined, Ravid pushed deeply into her mouth. There was no tasting, only conquest. His tongue demanded entry and took it in the slim moment of hesitation her pulsing body allowed him. His body was hard and solid with intent as he stroked her tongue with his.

Zeva ripped her mouth away and shoved at their chests. "No! I must return home!" With one hand on each warrior, she struggled to push her body back onto the bed. Each warrior was on either side of it and she ducked under their arms and rolled right over her own shoulder and off the edge of the round sleeping surface.

Her feet hit the floor with practiced balance. The tiny sign of her endless training hours gave her a spark of hope. Zeva pushed up and moved away from the dark forms in that bed. Her eyes tried to resist the image they made there. Part of her was delighted by the sight of aggression being aimed at her. In their eyes, she was desirable beyond any other female on the planet. It was more than the color of her skin or hair, Ravid and Keenan had caught her scent and somewhere inside both males...they approved of her. It was not something based on logic. Neither Keenan nor Ravid were thinking about it. This was reaction, pure and older than time, it moved through her bloodstream as her breasts ached.

Zeva shook her head. She was insane to even think about that. Ravid rose to his feet first and moved towards her. Even in the dim light, his body showed her a rigid stance, betraying his displeasure. His hand lifted towards her. "Come here, Zeva."

The door curtain moved and more light shot across the room. An older female entered without asking permission. She blinked her eyes as she took in the scene, before a little smile lifted her lips. She walked right in between Ravid and Zeva as she took Zeva's hand. "I am Elpida. Ravid is my son."

Zeva was grateful for the dim light because her face burned with color. Elpida moved over to the wall and ended even that little blessing by increasing the light level in the room. She considered Ravid and Keenan with knowing eyes before she aimed a smile at Zeva.

"I cannot wait to introduce you to Milena, Keenan's mother. She had given up hope that her only child would ever find a mate." Elpida turned to look at Ravid and the warrior snapped to attention under her gaze. It was that same manner of control that every parent wielded over their offspring...even when the son was a warrior who towered over his mother by a foot and a half.

"Her distress summoned us, Mother." Elpida nodded approval of Ravid's reason before she turned to look at the little bed once more. She sent a naughty smile at Zeva before turning back to look at her son. "That is understandable. But you should go have words with her brother, he waits below."

Ravid and Keenan couldn't disobey that. There was strict tradition to observe between warriors and maidens. Because she was still a maiden, their presence in her bedchamber tested the limits of what would be tolerated by the rest of the clan. The rules were all held in place by honor. An Alcandian male wasn't a warrior if he had no honor.

Ravid and Keenan nodded to her before they left. Zeva felt the parting deeply as she watched the curtain fall closed behind them. Her body lamented the growing distance and bitterly wailed at her to follow them.

Elpida laughed as she turned and aimed that naughty grin at Zeva once again. "That should remind them to consider your good name." Elpida clasped her hands together before she ran her eyes up and down Zeva. "Your mother will have my hair hanging on her chamber wall if I fail to chaperone you under my own roof."

That was certainly true enough. Zeva shook her head but smiled as she considered Paneil demanding Elpida's hair. Among Alcandian women, disputes were sometimes settled with the mother's hair being offered as an apology. Jett would never have left Zeva sleeping in a warrior's hall if a mature woman had not given her word to look after her.

That was also the only way to end a binding. A female could send her hair to her mates and refuse to live with them. It severed their legal union but not the mind-bridge that bound them. On Alcandar, a female only cut her hair in dishonor.

"You must be hungry, Zeva. Let us go to the women's hall for a meal. You should tell me what you like so that my son packs a good meal for your initiation supper."

Her mind said no but it was out-shouted by her body. Zeva shivered as she thought about her brother sitting with Ravid and Keenan. There was no turning back and there were far too many little temptations running through her for it to be a mistake. Whispers of the way Ravid touched her, rippled down her body as she remembered the taste of Keenan's kiss. Each male was unique and they were even more potent combined.

It looked like fate didn't bother to ask...she dealt her whims when and where she pleased. Zeva hissed as she felt the weight of need moving through her body. Frustration ate at her but she wasn't sure just why. Was it need for Ravid and Keenan or the desire to leave them behind?

\* \* \* \* \*

"I care not if you like it, Jett." Ravid gave in to his fury and didn't care for the glance Keenan aimed at him to temper his words. Zeva's taste clung to his lips and he wanted more. He needed to touch her, taste her…make her his.

"That was not my point, Ravid." Jett shook his head as he sat heavily on a bench. "My mother does not need to lose her daughter so soon again. You should have let my sister have time before approaching her."

"That was impossible." Keenan's voice was low but coated with determination. "Our minds had brushed, Jett, and her night-terrors summoned me as certainly as your own mate's distress would have done. There was no ignoring it. In truth, I will not rest well until Zeva is under my protection." Her nightmare still haunted him. Keenan frowned as her panic echoed in his head. He wanted to kill. Reach out and crush the throats of the men who had tried to break her sprit. They had no honor to practice their hate on a female. Even one they believed was from their enemy's side. War was fought between warriors.

"Your mother will not lose her daughter." This time Ravid spoke with a measure of soothing in his voice. Jett raised an eyebrow at him. Ravid didn't say anything further because he did not know what he could say. Jett was correct to believe that it would soon be much harder for Zeva's family to see her. That was a burden of his profession. It was something he and Keenan had accepted as the price for their dedication to Alcandian law.

Once you pledged your life to the Judgment ranks, mingling with other warriors became limited. As their binding mate, Zeva would have to follow them into that secluded form of Alcandian life. To remain in her current life could be dangerous. Ravid would not allow it, but it brought him no joy to see her fighting their union. He was proud of his dedication to duty—it defined who he was. Zeva's resistance to meet him before her abduction hit him personally. Defending the law was his life.

"We will make her happy, Jett. You should be more understanding of this. Your mating was not an easy union. But it is not a matter to debate, we have touched her mind and you sat here while we did it." Jett nodded and rose. He looked up at the half wall covered by a curtain and nodded approval. Everything was in order. He would have expected Ravid and Keenan to leave him in peace if it was his mind brushing with their sister's. When a warrior found his mate, he did not need any interference.

"I need to take my sister home. It is for her to inform her mother." Frustration tightened Jett's face but he held his thoughts and aimed a harsh glance at Ravid and Keenan. "My mother will expect your invitation before sunset."

Ravid growled. Keenan grunted in answer to the sound. Need burned through them both, setting them on edge. Life was never simple for a Judgment official but without Zeva, it would be impossible.

Keenan lifted his drink towards his companion. "Drink with me, brother. Soon, we will be complete."

"Aye." Ravid grinned as his body pulsed with need. Very soon he would feed the desire that twisted his thoughts. Keenan was correct, this was a moment to toast.

For tomorrow they would begin a new life that included a mate. For all three of them life would need to adjust and that would be the biggest challenge any of them had ever faced.

# Chapter Four

### ℰↄ

"We will go to Zanfelar!" Zeva frowned, her mother was beginning to worry her. Paneil swept into her room at dawn with three of her friends and the women were turning the place upside down.

"And then on to Ramothia. Get moving, Daughter! The day is wasting away."

Paneil stuffed things into a traveling case without even folding it. Her mother was normally so neat it broke her heart to see the careless way she handled things this morning.

It also made her furious to see the woman who had borne her, so frightened. Zeva stepped out of her bath and pulled the case from her mother's hands. Just wait until she got her hands on Ravid and Keenan. This was their doing!

"Mother, be at ease. You taught me to face my problems. I will not run. This is my home." Paneil broke into tears in response. Zeva fumed as she hugged her mother. Yes, she had a few things to say to a certain pair of Judgment officials! They would not turn her life upside down and even if they managed that, they would not distress her mother. "I have spent a year trying to return here." Zeva pulled a pair of pants on that her mother had missed and reached for the matching coat. It was her studio uniform and the clothing made her smile. Yes, she was home and she refused to leave. She would face Ravid and Keenan today and…well, she was not certain of exactly what would happen but her mother didn't need to be upset.

Her nipples tingled, making her frown. Shaking her head, she tugged a brush through her hair a little too fast. Her strands of hair protested and the pain banished the little zips of pleasure from her nipples. Her body was so aware it was almost frightening. She knew that mating brought pleasure but no one had ever mentioned that separation caused pain. The idea that Ravid and Keenan were now part of her life clashed with the years of self-sufficiency she had spent building her own life.

"I am going to class," she announced. "I will see you tonight, Mother. Tickle Sandor for me." Her new nephew was her mother's delight and Zeva smiled at her as Paneil gave her a long considering look. Her face broke into a smile as she clasped her hands together.

"You see? My daughter is made of solid confidence!" Paneil left with her friends as Zeva moved towards the doorway. Her bed shimmered and the wrinkled linens were gone with clean ones left in their place. Her body shuddered as the two dark shapes of her night visitors invaded her thoughts.

The visions refused to leave her alone. Her nipples rose into tight little buttons that begged for another night filled with the hard chests of her company. The aching tips yearned for the same hot kiss that her lips had tasted, and that desire spread down her belly until the little bud sitting at the top of her sex slowly pulsed with the same need.

She had to end this insanity! Her body had always been her tool. Training filled her thoughts from morning to night as she funneled her energy into building a studio that produced some of the finest females on the globe.

She refused to see her efforts melt into an inferno of lust. Yet it was more than lust and Zeva knew it. She faced the day with excitement twisting her body. Tonight she would be alone with them again. The day felt both too long and too short. Her passage ached for that deep touch she understood the realities of, but had never felt. Zeva understood the stark difference between male and female but today was the first time she had ever craved to use those differences.

She wanted to be filled. Have her body stretched by Ravid's and Keenan's harder ones. Her passage felt empty and the only thing she could think about was just how good Ravid and Keenan tasted.

But Ravid and Keenan? They would not touch, they would take and conquer. The two warriors loomed over her like a shadow. They grew longer and more massive each second she didn't turn around and force herself to see the object casting those dark shapes.

But looking them in the face showed her everything that her body craved.

\* \* \* \* \*

"Did I look that unhappy when I was binding with your brother?" Jessica stood in the doorway to Zeva's office and stared at her.

Zeva glared at her sister-in-law. "You were so angry, your face was red most of the time."

Jessica laughed and nodded her head. She shrugged her shoulders as she looked at Zeva. "Well, Dylan did kidnap me."

"And Jett?" Zeva truly wanted to know.

Jessica's eyes narrowed with remembered anger as she shot Zeva a harsh look. "Your brother never gave me a single morsel of information that I didn't flat out ask for. He left me completely in the dark and I swear he enjoyed watching me bump into walls."

"That can be summed up in the word 'warrior'." Zeva smiled because Ravid and Keenan both liked her to be the one reacting to them. Before she had gotten stuck on Earth, the two warriors had been carefully surrounding her, edging closer and pushing her into corners. Looking back, she didn't like what she saw. She had reacted to their pursuit like prey to a hunter. It was never something she thought too much about, instead she just turned to imprisoning herself on female grounds.

It was not the most mature thing to find in her past.

"So, what are you wearing tonight?" Jessica asked the question innocently but knew exactly what she was doing. Left on her own, Zeva would wear a uniform day in and day out. Zeva groaned and looked at Jessica. Her sister-in-law laughed before leaning across Zeva's desk to grab her hand.

"Come on, Zeva, picking out something pretty won't kill you, I promise."

Zeva followed Jessica and grumbled at her mother under her breath. Paneil was rather clever—there was nothing that Zeva detested more than picking out garments!

"It won't kill me but you might be tempted to." Jessica turned her head to look at Zeva and Zeva giggled. "Ah, what was that you said about Jett not offering any information until you collided with the hard fact? Well…like mother…like son."

Jessica groaned but pulled Zeva along to the garment viewing booth. "I should have known." She rolled her eyes. "Jett thought it was a very good idea."

* * * * *

"Find your daughter." Ravid issued his order over Jett's shoulder as he stepped between the warrior and his mother. Paneil propped her hands onto her hips and stepped around her son to poke the warrior in the chest with her finger.

"My daughter is not frightened of you." Her mother's voice was soaked with pride even if the image of her stabbing Ravid with her finger was really quite funny. Zeva felt her lips twitch into a little grin as Ravid towered over her mother's head.

The hall went silent as she appeared in the doorway. This was the men's hall of Sinlar and she didn't enter it often. Curious eyes moved over her as Ravid and Keenan both swung their full attention to her. Zeva held her head high as she moved into the room further.

Her eyes weren't quite as obedient to her wishes. They moved over the prime images of both warriors. Their maroon coats with the black edges looked enticing tonight instead of repulsive. The maroon fabric stretched over chests that were wide with muscles. Her fingertips tingled with the desire to rest against those torsos as she got close enough to smell their warm skin.

Zeva blinked her eyes and raised them to Keenan's. His lips rose in a grin as his eyes flashed at her. As she moved the final few steps towards him, his eyebrow rose with disbelief. "You came."

Her pride reared its head. "Of course. My mother has reared me correctly." There were a few nods from the surrounding warriors as Zeva felt Ravid step up next to her. She ignored the jump and shiver that raced through her spine.

Jessica moved toward Jett and shot Zeva a hard look. Zeva dropped the hand she had settled over her breasts. Ravid's and Keenan's eyes immediately dropped to the cleavage her action reveled.

Jessica grinned and shot Zeva an "I told you so" look. The long topaz coat with its low cut collar was Jessica's choice. The look on Ravid's and Keenan's faces declared Jessica the winner in that battle. Their eyes enjoyed the view of the tops of her breasts and it sent heat pouring down her spine.

Zeva shook her head and looked forward but the hall was not set for dinner. The first meal was always shared at the head table so that the female would not feel cornered or frightened by her intended mates. Keenan stepped forward and captured her hand in his. His skin was almost too hot as it closed around her fingers. Gooseflesh spread up her arm as she refused to think about how strong his grip felt.

"We will dine on Judgment grounds."

Zeva shifted back from his body but halted as Ravid moved behind her. Once more she felt surround by them and her lungs froze as she tried to ignore their hard presence. It was an impossible task but Zeva struggled to hold the surging sensation inside as she pressed her lips into a solid line. She focused on the distance between Keenan's body and her own. Tonight was another example of why she did not want to bind with Judgment officials. Taking binding vows was a major change for any female but doing so with Keenan and Ravid would be a radical alteration to her life.

Zeva looked at her mother as Paneil frowned. Keenan moved towards the door but Zeva stayed in place. He turned and raised an eyebrow at her.

"Is your mother so lax with her own daughters as to allow them to simply be swept out the door without a word? My mother is not." Zeva hadn't considered that tonight would take place someplace other than her own family grounds...but she should have. Jessica's words floated through her mind as she looked at the two warriors and their firm resolve to remove her to their territory.

Ravid's face flushed at her words. Anger flickered across his eyes but he controlled it and nodded at her. It was a concession and Zeva felt a surge of contentment hit her. Ravid was not a warrior used to softening his approach. He was a deadly male who performed his duties with swift strokes. Many warriors did not even dare to raise their voices to him.

Her eyes bulged as Ravid turned and gave her mother a half bow. "My apologies, *darmasha*." He moved on swift feet and clasped her mother's hand. He left a small marker behind. It was a data disk that held a communications link to the two-inch-wide wrist communicators both warriors wore.

Ravid aimed his eyes back at her and Zeva swallowed roughly. He was pleased with her. Power radiated from him like a solid wall. Zeva watched his hunger grow from the idea that she was in fact leaving with him and Keenan. The hardest part was feeling her own need rise under that heat.

Keenan captured her hand and swept her through the door in the next second. Zeva clutched at her confidence as they moved on those long strides towards a small transport. Four other warriors waited with it. The force field that covered the door was down and Zeva stepped right into the passenger compartment. She forced her body into the small space with sheer willpower. Her mind tried to transpose memories of splotch-colored uniforms instead of maroon ones.

The nightmare was unexpected and Zeva bit her lip to try and dispel it.

Trapped inside with Keenan and Ravid, Zeva struggled to breathe. Her senses were ultra-keen as little details appeared larger than life. Like Ravid's hands. They were large even by warrior standards. He sat across from her with his fingers curled into fists, and all she could think about was the way he used those hands to stroke her. It had been pure rapture. A little voice nagged her to let the warrior lay his hands on her again, this time without any fabric to interfere.

She shifted her eyes to encounter Keenan's huge frame. Both warriors sat facing her. It was only proper for them to share a seat and leave her alone while the first few days of their courting commenced. The Judgment officials riding in the transport behind them served as escort and witness.

Keenan's legs were amazing. She'd felt them last night and knew his pants hid pure perfection from her eyes. Sculpted and formed into solid strength, she imagined they would feel perfect twisting with hers.

Heat flared up her neck as Zeva forced a breath into her lungs. Strange how a few days of freedom could make her unable to deal with confinement. She had hidden her feelings for an entire year, yet panic was dragging her into its grip inside the transport.

Ravid growled and Zeva jumped. He reached across the seat and pried her fingers free of her jacket. Her hands had twisted the fabric into deep wrinkles on top of her thighs.

"Your fear is insulting, Zeva." Confusion fluttered across her face as Ravid held on to his temper. His jaw ached from the strain and he was near his breaking point. He was a warrior. No female was unsafe in his care. It was a matter of honor.

"I'm not afraid of you." Fighting with Ravid allowed her to breathe. Zeva tossed her head and tried to pull her hands free. Ravid held them in an iron grip as his thumbs slipped across the skin of her inner wrists. Pleasure zipped up her arms as he made little circles on the sensitive skin. A tiny gasp tried to escape her lips and Zeva tightened them to contain it.

Neither warrior believed her. Keenan studied the marks on her jacket before raising an eyebrow at her. "It is far past time you learned to accept us."

Zeva twisted her hands and broke Ravid's hold on her. The warrior looked stunned for a moment at the ease she regained her freedom. Pride lifted the corners of her lips as she sat back against her seat. She was a master of defense arts and on Alcandar, females needed to know how to break the much stronger grips of a warrior. There was a good reason that she was the master at her school—she knew her art well.

She crossed her hands over her chest to keep them away from the man but a single corner of his mouth rose in admiration. "Truly, you are a perfect match for us. Your defense skills will be well suited to the mate of Judgment officials."

"Aye." Keenan nodded approval, making Zeva gasp.

"Why?"

Ravid reached across the transport and captured one of her arms again. He moved like lightning and stretched her limb out in front of her eyes. This time his hand held hers much differently, she would have to move closer to his body to break the hold and his eyes dared her to try it. Goose bumps covered her skin from his touch and he stared at the telltale sign of response.

"Does it matter? You cannot hide your body's reaction to mine." Ravid's other hand found that same sensitive spot on her inner wrist and lightly rubbed it. Her arm jerked in response, making her gasp. A small smile appeared on his firm lips but it didn't reach his dark eyes. Zeva caught the flare of excitement in his eyes as he rubbed her inner wrist again. "You body is full of tender spots, Zeva, and I promise you I will touch each one."

The transport slowed and stopped, distracting her with the promise of freedom from the transport. Zeva dived through the door as the particle screen dissipated and Ravid was forced to release her hand or yank her arm from its socket. A deep grumble was his response as he let her wrist go.

Zeva filled her lungs with a deep breath and felt her shoulders relax. A little hum of delight caught in her throat as she viewed her surroundings. It was delightful. The mirror-smooth surface of a lake that reflected the light from the newly risen moon in front of her. The sound of moving water reached her ears as well as the chirp of night birds as they hunted.

The glow of two lanterns brightened a spot a few hundred feet from the road. There wasn't a table set for their meal. Keenan and Ravid had chosen a blanket spread on the soft mat of *hiutop* that covered the ground. Tiny lilac flowers dotted the sage leaves she stood on. With the lantern light and starshine it was a scene set for seduction.

That little voice inside her head nagged her to notice the attention to detail that had been done for her. The soft lighting and sound of moving water were feminine delights. Ravid and Keenan were not required to make such efforts for her. Yet she was grateful for the open surroundings. Now that she was free of the transport her body was releasing the tension being trapped inside it had produced.

Anger buzzed through her brain momentarily. The humans should not have been able to follow her back to Alcandar but it looked like they had planted little hooks into her that she needed to pry away before freedom was truly hers again.

Two large hands landed on her shoulders and firmly rubbed. Keenan's rich male scent drifted past her nose as she tilted her head to see his fingers moving on her right shoulder. Her nipples tingled as they rose into tight little buttons under her coat. The soft fabric cupped each mound, making her far too aware of how much she would like Keenan to handle her breasts. His warm breath hit her ears as he sighed and rubbed her shoulders again. "Truly, Zeva, I do not understand why you harbor such fear of warriors. Judgment officials are not so different from your own brother."

"I am not afraid of you." Zeva tried to step forward but the hands on her shoulders closed on her and held her in place. The heat from Keenan's body bled across the slight space he left between them as his scent teased her nose with the promise of how good he would smell when they were pressed together.

"Then why are your shoulders tightened into knots?" He snorted softly. He wasn't asking her a question. His words were a flat statement of judgment and her pride refused to accept it. Her mouth opened before common sense had the chance to protest.

"I don't like being locked up. The transport was too small. I felt like I was back on Earth. I shouldn't feel like that but I did." Zeva snapped her mouth closed because she hated the way her own words sounded. She wasn't weak and she did not want either warrior thinking she was fragile. The need to gain approval from both males grew until it overshadowed her need to keep the information hidden.

Zeva moved forward as Keenan's hands grew lax as he considered her words. All six warriors had heard her and deep frowns marked their faces. Zeva held her face in a smooth mask as she faced them. "It's no big deal. I'll get over it."

Zeva turned and walked away from the group. Her body lamented the distance, reminding her of how delightful Keenan's hands were.

Keenan growled and Ravid was the one to slap a hand on his companion's shoulder in warning. Keenan's eyes blazed with fury as Zeva's hips caught his attention. The sultry way her bottom swayed as she walked was ultrafeminine and it made him even more angry. What kind of a creature bred fear in a woman? Only a human would do something so deplorable!

Earth had too many females — it was the only reason their males treated them so poorly. Keenan had been raised to understand that he might someday need to search an alien world for his mate and possibly even abduct her, but he would never abuse her. Captive mates were handled with extreme care, Judgment officials always observed their treatment. If they could not adjust, their memories were shifted and they were returned to their homeworlds.

That was rare but it did happen.

But Zeva had resisted them for years. It had turned into a game that he and Ravid enjoyed too much. "It is time to decide this."

Ravid laughed softly, and two of the other warriors joined him. Zeva would not simply obey because they had decided it was time. There was part of him that enjoyed her need to challenge him. Maybe she needed to be run to ground, just to ensure that he was strong enough to do it. She might strike him for that idea but attraction wasn't governed by logic. It was born in the corners of the brain that were primitive and so the idea wasn't so unimaginable. Zeva was strong and her body would demand a superior mate.

The warriors split into two teams and walked off in different directions. Keenan didn't mind Zeva's current charade of calmness. Ravid did though. The current chase would be worth the wait. Zeva was here and Keenan didn't really care why she had joined them of her own free will, only that she had.

Zeva stopped as she looked at the smooth surface of the lake. Two pairs of maroon coats caught her vision as the warriors moved off into the distance. They would stay within sight and hearing. Heat burned her cheeks as she considered that. The warriors would not watch them but they were there for her comfort. An Alcandian woman was never left alone with intended mates on their first meal sharing. That was the reason most binding members ate in the men's hall—there were plenty of eyes and ears around to ensure that rape did not result from the raging binding fever.

Even the sleeping quarters of bound females were open to the inner eating hall. The rooms were built around the edges of the building on the second floor. The inner wall of each chamber was, in fact, a balcony, just a half wall that was open to the hall below. Sound flowed freely giving a mate further confidence that she was not cornered in a room with two large males who could overpower her.

Heat rushed over her skin as she thought about being in a chamber with Ravid and Keenan. More flames flickered across her body as she considered that the men standing slightly off in the distance fully expected to hear her cry out in pleasure tonight. It all combined in her belly and flowed down her... Zeva gasped as she recognized that her passage was full of heat. She had never been so aware of that tender female part of her body. Tonight she felt it pulse with sensation as fluid slipped down to the opening of her body.

"Zeva? Come and eat."

Her eyes moved to Keenan without her approval. Zeva scolded herself for looking at the warrior but her eyes didn't care. They moved over the prime picture of strength he made. She traced his lips as hers tingled with memory and longing. The heat rose into a wave that crashed into her body and filled her passage with need. A slight step behind her made her jump and she swung around with her leg already snapping out in a solid kick.

Ravid sent his body out of her path and ended up falling into the lake. Water rose from the warrior's huge body as it hit the smooth surface and Zeva landed in a perfect fighting stance. Ravid was sitting on his butt in the shallow water with an incredulous look on his face.

Water splashed onto her as Keenan choked behind her. It was a poor attempt to cover his amusement and Ravid snarled at his companion. Zeva covered her mouth with a slim hand as she caught the soft sounds of the attending teams' laughter. She backed up slightly as Ravid climbed to his feet.

"You really shouldn't sneak up on people. Keenan was talking to me and, well, I just didn't expect you to come up behind me." Her apology was ruined as a giggle escaped her hold on her emotions. Water dripped from Ravid as he stalked from the lake. Zeva spread her hands open in innocence. "It was pure instinct, Ravid."

The delight simmering in her eyes made it impossible to remain angry. Ravid felt it hit him in the solar plexus like a hard fist. This was the woman he was allowed to laugh with. There was a part of him that wanted to smile like a young boy just because he knew she would tease him back.

But the cock in his pants hardened painfully as he considered where play could lead with a fully grown woman.

Ravid snagged her wrist and Zeva squealed. Caught up in another round of giggling, the unexpected capture made it impossible to hold her surprise in. Ravid gave a swift tug on her arm and her body tumbled towards his dripping wet one. Zeva ducked under his arm and went splashing out into the swallows as she broke the grip on her wrist. Ravid turned on her with a devil's grin and crooked a finger at her.

"Come here, Zeva, I want to give you a hug."

"No, thank you!" She jumped back and her shoes slipped in the mud on the bottom of the lake. The water wasn't very deep but it rose to her knees as she tried to scamper around Ravid and back onto shore. The warrior stretched out his huge arms that were dripping water and prevented her from getting back onto the shore without moving within his reach.

Ravid grinned at her rejection. "Ah, Zeva, forgive me, I am wet." He reached for the two buttons at the waist of his coat, one on either side of his chest and snapped them open. He shrugged the wet fabric down his arms and tossed it onto the shore.

Zeva felt her lungs freeze. His chest was magnificent. Sculpted into ridges of solid strength. That heat returned with full force as it slammed into her body, making her ache for the same freedom from her own clothing. He crooked his finger at her again.

Zeva shook her head but couldn't quite force her mouth to form any words of rejection. Her body wanted to obey him and it took every last scrap of willpower she had to shake her head.

One dark eyebrow rose as his arms stretched out again. Ravid gave a low growl that made her shiver. This time the sound wasn't one of anger. It rumbled out of his wide chest proclaiming how strong he was...how male he was. Her passage actually clenched as she shifted away from him.

Her motion caught his attention. Ravid lunged after her and captured her body as she turned to run. His arms closed around her waist and he clasped her against his body. His face was pressed against her breasts as he walked out of the water.

"Keenan! I have caught a *deporth*." His steps made her head wobble, held above him as she was, and Zeva placed her hands on his shoulders to steady her body. Keenan laughed as Ravid brought her toward him. A *deporth* was a mythical chether born of starshine. Alcandian girls tossed flowers into lakes hoping a *deporth* would find the blooms pretty enough to grant them a wish that night.

"Then hold onto her, brother, else she will melt back into the water and be lost."

One of her shoes was pulled off her foot as Ravid reached the lantern light. Keenan tossed the wet ankle boot aside before he reached for the other one. The warm night air hit her bare toes as he rubbed the arch of her foot. Her pants were wet up to her knees but Keenan ignored them as Ravid lowered her to her feet. She was grateful he had left her pants on and knew it was done against his desire. Heat burned in Keenan's eyes as he leaned forward to gently inhale her scent. Neither warrior was actually touching her in that moment but she stood between their bodies with the heat from their skin teasing her bare arms. Her body shivered. The tremor shook her spine as her fingertips longed to touch Ravid's bare chest.

"We had best eat, Zeva."

Food did not interest her, but having Keenan's and Ravid's attention directed away from her body did. Her stomach was twisted into a knot as her eyes once again roamed over Ravid's bare chest. She lowered her lashes and sat down to avoid the arms connected to that chest. They were covered in more of the same perfection and her fingertips longed to smooth over the ridges.

Food appeared as Keenan pressed one of the small command compression areas on his wrist link. Ravid still wore his as well—Judgment officials never took them off. They were specially formed to allow the skin beneath to breathe. Three large platters of food appeared with steam rising from them. Wormhole technology was useful in many ways. Keenan could place the order for food and have it delivered at the touch of a command key. The food would wait in stasis and never grow cold until it materialized.

Zeva pulled a piece of food from a plate and put it in her own mouth. The action was rude but she couldn't stop the nervous habit. Her body was too full of strange longings tonight.

Keenan caught her wrist an inch from her lips and turned her hand towards his face. His fingers closed around hers making her hold onto the food as he brought his lips down to it. His lips closed over her fingertips as he nipped the food out of her grip. He held her hand as he chewed the food before he opened his mouth to gently suck the remaining sauce from her fingers. His tongue left her skin as he growled. "Sweet."

Zeva jumped and would have stood up except Ravid's arm was over her folded legs. If she moved she would collide with his bare chest again. She sucked in a deep breath as she fought for control. This was madness! But she craved it.

Zeva grabbed another piece of food and offered it to Ravid. They could not touch her body first, only her hands, so she had to keep her body still and feed them. If she moved into Ravid's body, he was allowed to embrace her because she had touched him first.

There was something raging inside her to tempt them beyond their control. Push the limits of how long she might hold them away from her. Zeva fought her own need as the smell of their skin made her ache for much deeper contact than fingers to lips.

It was a game of temptation. One that tested the trust of a female for her intended binding mates. They enticed and waited until she succumbed. Ravid's bare chest made her shiver as he bit into the food in her hand. He took only half the bite and slowly chewed it. Her eyes flickered over the arm he had braced over her legs as she tried to keep her attention on the task at hand. His bare skin made it nearly impossible and Zeva struggled to hide her growing fascination with his chest.

Both males could discard their clothing whenever they wished, that was part of the temptation. She was bound only to have bare arms and hands for this first official courting meeting. At the next, though, they held the right to inspect her nude body.

Ravid's mouth closed around her fingers as he took the last of her offering. He chewed the food and didn't release her hand. His fingers closed around hers as he stroked the center of her palm while watching her eyes. He offered her a taste of the meal as he pulled her hand closer to his body to keep her close to him. She had turned away from Keenan before he could feed her in return.

Her throat contracted. There was too much heat twisting in her belly for food. The scent of the meat actually made her nauseous as her stomach violently refused to have anything in it.

Ravid's eyes closed to slits as his lips pressed into a firm line of disapproval. Zeva didn't offer any reason for her refusal to eat—all her reasons sounded weak and she refused to voice them. She did not understand her body at that moment and decided to simply not try. "I am not hungry."

*For food.*

Her hand fell the last inch to his forearm and smoothed up its corded length. A sigh of delight filled the air as she moved that hand all the way to Ravid's shoulders. Zeva couldn't stop her hand, he felt too good. Skin to skin made her shiver with pleasure.

Ravid's expression instantly changed. He dropped the food and caught the side of her face with his hand. His mouth landed on hers as Zeva surged off the blanket.

His lips pushed hers open as she backed into Keenan. Two hands landed on her shoulders in response. A moan caught in her mouth as Ravid took a deep taste from her lips and Keenan moved towards his companion, pressing her towards that bare chest. Her fingertips demanded contact with Ravid's skin. At that moment she couldn't think beyond the knowledge of how close Ravid was to her. His mouth took hers and filled her senses with his taste. She needed to touch him. Feel how strong he was and let that knowledge mingle with the taste of his kiss.

Ravid's chest rumbled with approval as her hands gently touched him. It was almost a whisper of a brush—skin against skin, as Zeva used only her fingertips to test how warm his male flesh was.

Pure sensation poured through her fingers and into her hands. It shot up her arms as gooseflesh rose around each tiny nerve ending. Her nipples tightened unbearably as she tore her mouth from Ravid's and panted. She was too hot and her lungs couldn't get enough air into them.

"Touch me, *ruthima*." It was another demand but her temper didn't rise to challenge it. Instead her fingers slid over his collarbones until they found his shoulders. Her palms joined the connection as she cupped each shoulder and found the corded muscles where they began their length down each of his arms.

She had to stop…this was pure madness.

Keenan turned her head as her eyelids fluttered and lifted. His blazed at her before his mouth touched hers. It was a light touch of male lips, gently tasting hers and testing the smooth surface of her mouth before she opened her lips to invite a deeper kiss.

Keenan did not disappoint her. His mouth pressed hers open as his hand cupped the side of her head and held her in place for his kiss. He deepened the contact as his tongue stroked the length of hers, slowly introducing her to the feel of their mouths mating.

Zeva threaded her fingers through Keenan's hair but left one hand on Ravid as she found herself craving both men. Her passage twisted again and this time she knew that the only answer to the craving was the two warriors touching her. She needed them closer as the heat grew more intense. It burned away everything but the three of them. Pleasure broke through her uncertainty as Keenan stroked her tongue once more.

Ravid cupped her breast. Even through her jacket the contact was jarring. Zeva gasped as she jerked away from Keenan to stare at Ravid. His eyes burned into hers as his fingers cupped her breast and gently squeezed it. "You like that, Zeva. The pleasure dances across your eyes."

She did but felt exposed under his burning gaze. Ravid moved his hand until he stroked the bare upper swell of that same breast. She gasped with pleasure as his lips lifted in a

smug grin. But there was more in his eyes than conquest—
Ravid wanted to see her pleasure.

Her lungs were pulling air in too fast to reply. Instead she
listened to her own whimper as his fingers released and his
thumb passed over her nipple. The hard nub exploded with
pleasure as it begged for freedom from her clothing. There was
a twin plea from her other nipple and a deep pulsing from her
passage. Pressed between the folds of her sex was another
swollen nub that clamored for attention.

Ravid could smell her arousal. It drove his into a frenzy
as he battled for control. His cock tightened further,
threatening to spill its seed from the scent of her wet body
alone. The sight of her bare breasts was going to drive him
insane but he was powerless to resist the urge to willingly
proceed to his own doom.

His thumb moved over her nipple again as sweat covered
his forehead. "Show me your body, Zeva. Let me taste this
nipple."

*Oh yes!*

A moan was the best her pride did to drown out her
hungry flesh. Keenan caught her head and found her neck
with his lips. New fingers of flames shot down her body into
her breasts and she just didn't care. She needed Ravid to free
her from her jacket. She wanted to burn the uncomfortable
garment so that it could never torment her skin again. Keenan
stopped at the collar and Zeva moaned as the garment kept
him from going any further. "I am going to open your jacket,
*shihori.*"

Her hands didn't want to leave Ravid's arms. She moved
them over his biceps as her eyes closed. Pure pleasure floated
around her. Keenan shifted and there was a slight popping
sound as he opened the two waist buttons on her jacket. The
night air was blissfully cool as it stroked her breasts.

A harsh sound of male approval made her lift her eyelids.
Ravid's face was harsh as he looked at her breasts. Her
confidence wavered as she saw his eyes flicker over her

nipples. Her breasts were large for her frame. Often she bound them when teaching because they distracted her. Until tonight she had never really thought about whether or not they were attractive breasts. They were just part of her body.

Keenan's hands cupped each globe and she shivered. Pleasure surrounded each breast as Ravid licked his lower lip. Zeva watched the fascination hold his attention as Keenan gently lifted her breasts and brushed the nipples with his thumbs. No hint of jealousy interfered in the moment. Ravid was enjoying the moment of shared delight. Keenan could feel her breasts as he took the first look at them. Caught between them, her body rejoiced.

Ravid's arms encircled her waist. He slid his hands over her bare skin and pulled her towards him as Keenan let her breast go. Keenan caught the edges of her open jacket and pulled the garment down her arms as Ravid bent to capture a nipple with his lips. The warrior lifted her up with his powerful arms and bent her over them, thrusting her breasts up for his mouth to feed on.

Keenan moved even closer until she could see his eyes watching her and Ravid. A harsh cry escaped her mouth as Ravid sucked her nipple into his mouth. Heat blazed over the tight button making her body convulse. Pleasure shot down her core as she gripped his head to hold him in place. She wanted him to keep sucking on her breast and she bent her back even further to offer it to his attention.

"You taste delicious," Ravid growled as he trailed his lips across her chest to her other nipple. He shifted and caught her legs with his arm to lift her completely from the ground. Her nipple popped free as Ravid knelt and laid her on the blanket. Ravid moved until her back rested against his chest and Keenan stroked her thigh with his firm hand.

Keenan pressed her legs apart as Ravid cupped her breasts and rolled her nipples between his fingers.

Her cry hit the night as Keenan rubbed his hands over her hips. The need to move her bottom coursed though her. One of

Keenan's hands stroked over her belly and she lifted her hips towards it.

Heat consumed her as Ravid pulled on her nipple without any hint of stopping. Keenan stroked her belly and moved to the top of her sex. Her passage ached as he stopped just at the very top of her mons. Her hips jerked upwards seeking the touch of that hand as Ravid returned to her opposite breast.

Her hands were tightened onto Ravid's arms as Keenan answered her body's plea. He sent his hand over her sex as his thigh lifted to spread her legs further apart. His fingers barely touched her clit before she convulsed with pleasure. He rubbed her mons and her bottom lifted for him. Everything twisted tighter inside her passage as she ached for the hard thrust of his male body.

Despite the fabric of her pants, her body jerked and shattered in a storm of sensation that caused her passage to contract.

"I-I can't...breathe!" Zeva shoved at her companions but they held her between their bodies as they stroked her. Her heart felt too large in her chest as it expanded and pumped frantically.

"*Ruthima,*" Ravid muttered against her hair as he smoothed her head onto his shoulder. Keenan's hand still rested on her sex as he firmly refused to release it as she wiggled. He watched her face as he stroked her sex a few last times. He moved his hand up her belly and over her bare breast to cup her jaw and smooth her neck with its pulsing artery. His cock throbbed with need and he enjoyed the bite of hard arousal. The scent of her wet body promised him satisfaction, and very soon.

"Now you see, *ruthima.* Your body was meant for us to master."

Zeva's eyes flew open as her senses stopped whirling. She surged to her feet and stood over Keenan before she found her voice. "Master?" She growled the word as her arms crossed over her chest to hide her breasts. A wave of liquid satisfaction washed through her as she stepped away from the two warriors. They pushed to their feet as she retreated once again.

"I will not be owned."

Ravid frowned darkly at her. "Yet I will master you, Zeva. Mating is not soft, it is primal and I will conquer you. You crave it as much as I do." His nostrils flared as he flexed his fingers and moved towards her. "Admit it."

"Not tonight." Their eyes battled as Ravid's mind linked with hers. His desire was raw and she found it intoxicating. "Take me back to my mother." She said it to taunt him. Her voice rose high enough to carry to the warriors who watched them. Ravid could not refuse to honor her request and Zeva enjoyed that moment of being the one to master Ravid. Her conscience warned her that it was just one skirmish in a long war but the sparks shooting from Ravid's eyes made her crave more engagements with him.

The warrior snarled as Keenan stepped into his path. One hand halted his motion as Keenan locked eyes with his brother. Keenan turned his eyes to hers and she shivered at the male she saw there. Keenan was no longer calm or patient. His glare promised her retribution.

Her stomach flipped over as she witnessed the fury burning in Keenan's eyes. He let her see the emotion before nodding his head.

"Very well, Zeva, tonight you bind us with tradition." Keenan lifted his hand from Ravid's chest and pointed a single finger at her.

"Tomorrow night, I will enjoy returning the favor."

# Chapter Five

## ℘

Zeva was distracted. She pulled a deep breath into her chest and felt her lungs expand completely. As she exhaled, her eyes opened and she pushed her foot off the mat.

Her body cut through the afternoon like a knife. Swift…precise…and unburdened. She landed perfectly balanced and pulled another deep breath into her lungs.

Her mind was at peace. Both Keenan's and Ravid's displeasure stared back from her last memory of them.

Actually, it was hard promise that they had shot at her. A smile attempted to lift her lips as she shook her head at her own emotions. Wherever the need to bait Ravid and Keenan had come from, she would do far better without it.

Still…it persisted.

Rolling her shoulders, Zeva left her mat and went towards a shower. Her body glistened with sweat and her muscles ached just the right amount. Her mind was always clear after a workout. When you pushed your body to its limits, the mind did not have time to intrude with its thoughts.

Ravid had the right to be cross with her—she had used her mother's name like a shield.

She sighed as she pulled her uniform off. Her skin was still sensitive. Little memories floated across her mind of the way she felt between the two warriors. The way Keenan touched her neck, the heat of Ravid's mouth on her nipple. The mirror showed her a body that was different from the woman who had left this studio just the day before.

Her neck was marked with little red marks from Keenan's teeth. She couldn't recall any pain from the bites. Her breasts were the most changed though. They felt different now. Fuller, and she was so much more aware of how sensitive they could be. In Ravid's hands, her breasts could transform her into a wanton creature who existed only for pleasure. The image of her twisting between the two warriors was wickedly tempting even in the bright light of day. Her passage still ached, complaining about how empty she felt.

Zeva was no fool. She knew what she craved. Her hip had rested against Keenan's swollen cock last night and her body delighted in reminding her of how hard he had been. A very different sort of ache would be keeping her company this morning if she had let her body lead her forward last night.

Her nipples tingled as they tightened further. Cupping her breasts with her own hands, Zeva rubbed her thumbs over her nipples as she watched her reflection. The sensation was pleasant but not shattering. She didn't crave her smaller...feminine hands.

What she craved was Keenan and Ravid.

\* \* \* \* \*

Ravid stopped pacing as a dramatic female sigh hit his ears. He turned on Amin but the female fluttered her dark eyelashes at him instead of scurrying away. She lifted a slim hand and wiggled all her fingers at him.

"That will do you no good with me. You forget, Ravid, I was bound to your brother. I believe I am immune to that particular growl." She blew him a kiss. "Now if you smiled at me, I might become concerned."

Ravid shook his head a second before Amin's son attacked his leg. The four-year-old let out a battle cry before punching his thigh with every ounce of strength his little body held. Ravid peeled his nephew off his leg before he had a limp to explain to Zeva.

A pair of dark eyes exactly like his brother's smiled at him as he lifted Kendrick onto his shoulders. It was moments like this that he truly had to face the fact that his brother was dead. When he looked into Kendrick's eyes he saw his brother looking back.

Ravid grinned as the boy climbed onto his normal place. Amin watched with a mother's eye as her son found a stable perch on his uncle's shoulder. Ravid was grateful to her at that moment. He couldn't remain angry with Kendrick around and he suspected Amin knew that.

"Did I drive Chandler as insane?"

There was another thing Ravid was often stunned by — Amin spoke freely of both her mates while he hesitated to speak their names around her. Love still crossed her eyes but she found comfort in talking about her deceased mates.

Fury still surged into his mind when his brother's name was mentioned. Chandler had been struck down by a coward's attack. His brother's killer was still free while his widow clung to memory instead of her mates. "I will enforce judgment on them."

"Stop it, Ravid. You will drive me to tears. It is time to move on." Amin stood up and shook out her coat. Ravid frowned as he noticed the way the top hung off her shoulders. His sister-in-law was a sack of bones now. "I did not reproach you for longing for Zeva for an entire year, so do not begrudge me my memories. Love does not make sense. It just is."

"I did not say I loved Zeva."

Amin giggled as she reached for her son. "You will understand in time, Ravid. It's what you don't say that matters. Love grows in stages you know. Right now desire drives you but when those flames die down a bit you will see that the true gift of a mate is the love that binds you together after your bodies have been satisfied."

Keenan aimed a confused look at Ravid over Amin's head. She eased her son to his feet and then followed him as the boy pulled her away while pointing at a passing plate of sweets. The warrior's hall was full of activity and females for a change. Tonight was their pledging ceremony and women hustled about arranging tables to their satisfaction. He and Keenan simply attempted to endure it. Their presence was demanded by the reigning dictators of the event.

Their mothers.

Keenan's mother was in the kitchens and Ravid's was at the head table. Both women looked engulfed in their work but they always noticed the second either he or Keenan tried to slip out of the hall.

Keenan sighed as he clasped his arms behind his back again. He lifted a blond eyebrow. "Do you love Zeva?"

"I need her." So badly it burned. Ravid looked at the activity surrounding him and willed it to move faster. Tonight, the three of them had to publicly announce their freedom. It was a tradition reaching back millennia on Alcandar. Zeva was a maiden and he and Keenan would declare their intentions to bind with her in order to protect her virtue. Even if they did not bind, she would not be regarded as an immoral woman for having shared intimacies with them.

And Ravid certainly intended to share a whole lot more with her than they had last night! Tonight, they would take Zeva to their chamber and there would be no running for her.

She would not leave his chamber as a maiden.

Keenan nodded but said nothing. He wasn't certain of his own feelings. Need poured over him like water every time he saw Zeva and it was soaking into him deeper every day. He wasn't willing to think about life without her any longer. It was a hard thing to accept. He had carved his life out of harsh odds that should have seen him fail. Judgment officials had the lowest odds of finding mate. Their dedication to duty kept them away from questing for a female that they could touch minds with.

It astounded him that they had found Zeva. He still marveled at the burn of their binding fever. Love seemed a great deal more to ask for in the face of such a great gift. Maybe it was too much.

Envious stares moved over him and Ravid as the hall began to fill with their fellow Judgment officials. Many of them had dedicated their lives to the maroon uniforms they wore. The only females they ever held were pleasure-givers—the few Alcandian women who were widowed and free to indulge their sexual needs with warriors who had never brushed the mind of a mate. It was an imperfect solution but common among Judgment officials. These warriors spent their time tracking law-breakers and that did not leave much time for their personal quests.

Love? Longing for it was one thing but expecting it was too much to hope for.

Keenan grinned. Insurmountable odds had never kept him from winning before. The image of Zeva's eyes sparkling with love made his heart jerk. Aye, the odds did not matter, only that there was a chance of success.

\* \* \* \* \*

"They are pledging tonight." Helmut waited to see what Craddock had to say. The other warrior stopped his workout and stood up. He flexed his shoulders before letting out a roar. His fists hit his chest as Helmut smirked.

Craddock rubbed his cock through his pants as it began to twitch to life. It had been a long time since he had taken a female and his seed needed release. But he wanted a female worthy of his seed.

"Let them taste her." Craddock aimed his hate-filled eyes at Helmut. "I want Ravid and Keenan to remember what her body felt like under theirs when I send her hair to them."

Insane laughter filled the crumbling house as Craddock rubbed his hard erection. Females were spoils and he intended to be the victor in his battle with Ravid and Keenan.

* * * * *

Excitement made her nervous but Zeva enjoyed the feeling tonight. Her robe was thin but her skin still protested the confinement. She slipped into a pair of soft, beaded slippers and frowned. She would rather be barefoot.

A sigh greeted the women helping her dress. Zeva didn't explain her mood—she was not certain she could make it understood.

She felt twisted with indecision, pulled towards tonight's ceremony, and away at the same time. Ravid and Keenan would take her into their world where her life would become part of theirs. Yes, they would be making adjustments for her as well but hard facts didn't always calm emotions.

Tonight her feelings ruled her, refusing to allow her brain to sift out fact from reaction.

Because they were Judgment officials, there were too many unknowns for her to wonder about. Telling herself they were just warriors wasn't working. It went beyond their clothing. Warriors spent years becoming enforcers of law. It was not a rank bestowed lightly or quickly. A warrior was expected to give freely of his time, discarding any and all things that did not belong to Judgment issues.

Ravid and Keenan were dedicated warriors and maybe that's what made her sigh. There was much in each male to appreciate.

"Daughter, it is time." Paneil looked at her with indecision on her face. Her mother still was not certain what to make of her mood.

Zeva took a look at her reflection. Tonight, Keenan would be pleased. Her jacket was low cut and her breasts swelled over the neckline. Moving her head, she watched the dark strands of her hair move and grinned. That should satisfy Ravid. Only two little pins held her long hair out of her eyes. It all cascaded down her back to her hips.

"I'm ready, Mother." Paneil smiled so widely her eyes crinkled almost closed. She proudly took her daughter's hand and led her down the stairs and out of the women's hall. The path was lined with girls too young to attend tonight's ceremony. They sighed as Zeva passed, with visions of their own binding dancing through their imaginations.

The path changed color as they stepped onto Judgment grounds. Elpida waited for Paneil to finish bringing her forward as another woman stood beside her. The other woman would be Keenan's mother.

Elpida and Milena stood with stern faces as they waited for Paneil to turn her around for their inspection. It was an old custom but one still practiced here on Judgment grounds. The two mothers could even demand Zeva be bared for inspection before they would allow her to be presented to their sons. A wicked smile tugged on her face as Zeva contemplated the fact that her mother could demand the exact same thing from Ravid and Keenan. Excessive modesty was certainly not an Alcandian trait but she rather hoped that her mother would leave the two warriors clothed. She was having enough trouble keeping her mind off Ravid's chest as it was.

Both mothers smiled as Paneil completed her circle and each hugged her mother. Their next embrace was offered to her.

"Welcome daughter, I am Milena. Keenan is my son." Milena was as fair-haired as Keenan.

"Blessings Zeva." Zeva turned to embrace Elpida as Paneil watched with a glowing face. Both mothers nodded their approval before Paneil took her hand and led her forward again. This time Milena and Elpida walked behind them to signify that she met with their approval.

It would be so simple to become terrified in that moment. In front of her, the path was lined with more girls too young to attend tonight's gathering. The difference was, these were the daughters of Judgment officials. They lived on even more secluded grounds than normal Alcandian females. Around each of their right wrists was an inch-wide silver band. Those bracelets marked them as Judgment children and also held location beacons to further protect them.

Zeva shivered as she forced her eyes to move to the sparkling eyes of those girls. Ravid and Keenan would clasp one of those bands on her arm during their binding ceremony if she showed up. Only Judgment officials could remove the bracelets.

Her heart gave an odd twist as they moved towards the warrior's hall. They led her across another boundary and maroon coats lined the path. There were so many of them that Zeva hesitated. These were Ravid's and Keenan's peers. She did not want to shame them in front of their friends. The two warriors deserved more respect than that.

"Oh Zeva, they are handsome warriors." Her mother patted her hand as they stopped at the doorway and looked into the main hall. Zeva felt her breath freeze as she glimpsed the sight awaiting her. Keenan and Ravid were the definition of prime. Handsome did not do them justice. Pride shot through her as she realized that the two warriors were waiting for her.

The next emotion that hit her made her shiver. Keenan and Ravid had not just waited for her, they had chased her. These warriors did not just want a mate, they wanted her and that idea warmed her as she felt their eyes on her. The feeling pushed right past her well-thought-out decisions and carved a hole in the wall she'd built with her logic.

Her and only her. Trust sprang up from that truth as she walked closer and closer to the two warriors. She might fear the lifestyle they would drop over her but she could never fear them. Trust wasn't something you made the decision to give to someone, it was born in your thoughts without consideration.

Surprise flashed through Ravid's eyes as she lifted her chin and stepped forward. Keenan's lips were set into a half grin as her mother handed her hand into his. Zeva watched his eyes as his fingers closed around hers in a firm grasp. Paneil placed her left hand in Ravid's grip and the hall exploded with applause.

Zeva wanted to bolt but two firm squeezes on her hands made her fight for the poise to stand in place. Her chest felt like a weight was sitting on it as the *yedith* stepped forward. The hall was silent as the older man looked at each of them before asking for their vows.

"Do you come to this binding free of vows to others?"

Keenan's voice was firm as he answered. Ravid stared at her as he answered the same question. His dark eyes probed hers as he drifted into her thoughts. He did it easily now. A wave of nervousness hit her as she recognized just how completely their thoughts could merge now.

Ravid gave her hand a sharp squeeze and she turned her head towards the *yedith*. His silver eyebrow was raised and the hall silent behind her.

"Yes."

The hall erupted into applause, saving her from speaking further. Keenan turned them to face the assembled group and Ravid stepped up close to her body. He kept her hand imprisoned in his grasp as he leaned down.

"You are plotting something, *ruthima*."

"I'm here, aren't I?"

He growled softly in her ear and a quick look from her lowered lashes showed Zeva a grin that chilled her. Ravid always played to win and it was a game of complete and total surrender. "Yes, you are. Yet you are still plotting, I feel it."

Zeva stabbed her thumbnail into his palm. A low chuckle was her response as the warriors began to seat themselves for the celebration dinner. Zeva tried to turn around and take her seat but Ravid held her hand and pulled it slightly around his hip to draw her close to his body.

Zeva looked into his dark eyes and grinned. "Holding grudges, Ravid? Last night had to end sometime."

Her nipples tightened as the scent of his warm male skin hit her senses. Her eyelids fluttered as she failed to resist the urge to scan his wide chest. Beneath that coat there was pure— Zeva stomped her foot to stop her wondering thoughts. She winced as her little slippers failed to protect her from the stone floor.

But Ravid's dark eyes sparkled with amusement as she managed to lift her eyes to look into his. His deep voice even sounded playful and Zeva stared at him in wonder. "Yes, and tonight needs to begin sometime."

"I am starving." Zeva tried to move towards her seat but Ravid held her in place. His lips twitched up into a grin as his thumb stroked the center of her palm. His eyes went deadly serious as she raised hers to them again. He lowered his head slightly and her back bent away from his towering height out of pure instinct.

"I claim the right of inspection."

"You would." Zeva whispered her words for Ravid alone. Her temper flared up bright enough to mask the heat being so close to his body produced. Zeva didn't know where passion and anger separated and she did not care.

She yanked on her hand, forcing Ravid to release her or hurt her. His fingers opened and she sprang back from his body. Keenan reached for her arm but she jumped out of the way as the room went silent again. "Inspection" was being whispered across tables as conversations abruptly ended and every pair of eyes returned to them once again. She looked at Keenan to end Ravid's game but her other intended mate crossed his arms across his chest before stating in his firm tone, "Agreed."

Paneil gasped as she stood up. Jett towered over her shoulder with a dark frown marring his face. Elpida cast a horrified look at her son but Ravid didn't appear to care. While inspection was an Alcandian tradition, it was not a common one and it insinuated that the bride's mother was hiding something from the grooms' mothers.

Ravid's dark eyes burned with challenge, his audacity had nothing to do with their mothers...it was completely personal. But the warrior had a lesson coming if he thought she would bend to his will.

"Very well." Zeva shot a warning look at Keenan before she walked down the aisle to where her mother stood. Paneil was turning red with anger as she stopped to squeeze her mother's hand. "Enjoy your meal, Mother. I do not need you."

Zeva moved down the aisle with her head held high. Elpida and Milena stood up and followed her because females inspected females before any male was ever allowed to do so. Ravid and Keenan were forced to wait until their mothers returned for them because Zeva had relieved her own mother of the inspection ceremony. Since they were already pledged, Milena and Elpida were now considered family and Zeva could let the bride-escorting duties fall to them.

That meant Ravid and Keenan were required to stand and wait. They could not enter their chamber until the mother escorting the bride returned to signal that they felt the bride was ready for inspection. Zeva could feel Ravid's frustration as she walked up the aisle with her head high. Ha! She doubted the arrogant warrior had believed she'd leave him in front of his peers!

Not to mention her family.

Zeva stopped at the back of the hall because she had no idea where to go. Stairs rose up from both corners of the building but she didn't know where Ravid and Keenan slept.

Doubt broke through her temper as she recognized that payback was indeed harsh. Last eve she had left them bound by tradition. Zeva shook her head as she followed Elpida. This binding fever truly brought out the worst in her.

Guilt slammed into her as she walked into the sleeping chamber. Her cheeks turned pink as she caught the embarrassed looks on Elpida and Melina's faces. The two mothers clearly hadn't expected their sons to cast any doubt on her worthiness to bind.

Zeva undid her clothing quickly and dropped it all over a chair. Elpida and Milena didn't waste anytime, they strode right past her to the curtain that covered the doorway and left without looking at her bare back. Zeva was not even sure they looked at her front.

Their voices came through the curtain. "Just wait until I get my hands on that child of mine."

"We should sit right here and make them wait until sunrise."

"I would do just that if I did not know they would spoil our game by coming up here." Elpida snorted. "Besides, we cannot leave Paneil below."

Zeva stuffed her fist into her mouth to keep her laughter from reaching their ears. There was some unspoken bond between mother and child. Even when that child was a full-grown warrior, a mother refused to relinquish her authority. The idea of Elpida taking Ravid to task made her walk away from the curtain before her amusement became too loud to cover.

The window screens were all off, letting the night air flow in. The lights had brightened as she walked in and Zeva passed her hand over the wall controls to lower them a bit. She wasn't hiding in the dark, just hesitant to stand in full light.

The chamber was more plush than she might have imagined it to be. Alcandian homes were covered in tile because it was lazered clean each morning by the main computer. Ravid and Keenan had deep area rugs that her toes sank into. A little hum of delight came from her throat as she tested one with a single foot. It was completely possible that the comforts had been added for tonight. The single round bed most certainly was. Unbound warriors did not share a bed but the three of them would.

Candles flickered with romantic welcome and blossoms were scattered over the furniture. One of the bedside tables held three drinking goblets placed there for her comfort. There were little details carefully placed throughout the chamber that made her reconsider her harsh views.

Warriors who wanted only to own her would not bother to seduce her. Tradition would give them the right to bring her into their bed. Zeva lifted a blue flower from the shimmering bed and inhaled its delicate fragrance. The idea of Ravid placing it among the bedding hit her with a wave of tenderness so large she tumbled off balance as it washed right into her heart.

There was also a window seat. Zeva secretly adored the things. She had never justified spending the funds to have one put into her own chamber but she climbed up onto the cushion and leaned over the edge to see the view. The candles sitting on the ledge flickered as the night air rushed into the room.

Ravid and Keenan found her like that. Zeva didn't hear them, she felt them. A mind-bridge was forming between them that would add to their physical intimacy. She felt their eyes move over her back and hair. The night air flowed in and across her breasts, cooling the heat that flickered to life inside her.

She was getting used to the combustion. In her passage, fluid coated walls that told her how sensitive they were. Tiny nerve endings in her skin clamored for the firm touch of male hands. It went beyond desire now, she needed to stomp on her pride and follow her body towards relief.

Her heart joined the melody as it tempted her with visions of seduction. There was no doubt where the night would end, but there was a part of her that craved it to be hours filled with enjoyment instead of pride-fueled clashing. Heat moved over her skin as Keenan's scent drifted to her nose. Desire built as she took a deep breath and savored the pure maleness of that scent. At that moment she didn't want to be on equal footing. Zeva wanted to be female, and her mates, warriors. They were vastly different but together their bodies could be complete.

Ravid stepped forward and Keenan thrust his arm out to halt him. He shot his companion a hard look before he took the lead this time. Zeva still hadn't moved. She knew they were there and simply sat. It was a humbling moment. Approval filled his thoughts as he saw her there. Just sitting in their chamber. All of the details fell aside as her delicate feminine scent drifted to his nose.

Keenan took a deep breath and let his blood surge through his body. He slid his eyes over the dark mane of hair covering her back and enjoyed the pulsing jerk of his cock. Arousal had ruled him too long but tonight he was content to enjoy the bite of it because Zeva was not leaving his chamber.

It was only a partial victory. Keenan moved forward and caught the slight tensing of her fingers. His frown deepened as he considered her unmoving body. Conflict, he understood. There was even a part of him that relished battling with Zeva. Her silent compliance was deafening.

She could smell him. Zeva was slightly astounded that she knew both warriors' scents. Her brain began thinking on a different level as she caught a second lungful of Keenan's scent. The fingers she had curled around the ledge of the window demanded she let them explore Keenan's chest just as she had Ravid's. She wanted to touch and be stroked in return. The wall of details separating them rubbed her raw as her body burned for theirs, and suddenly Zeva just didn't want to wait any longer. She always went after what she wanted and tonight was no different.

She stood up on the window seat and turned around. Keenan's body tensed slightly in response and she took advantage of the half second of shock. Slipping her hands over each side of his head she leaned forward to kiss him.

His mouth instantly opened as she sent her tongue towards his. Zeva pushed her body towards the warrior and he caught her weight as she stroked the length of his tongue. A harsh groan shook the chest she clung to as his arms tightened around her.

"That is the last time I allow you to go first, Keenan."

Zeva broke their kiss and looked past Keenan to Ravid. His eyes flashed with desire as he watched them. Keenan's hand was fisted in her hair as the warrior held her completely off the ground. Her hands were curled over his two massive shoulders as she looked over one of them. Ravid's dark eyes flashed again as they locked with hers and he pulled his jacket off.

Zeva listened to her own little gasp as she once again caught sight of his chest. Keenan lowered his mouth to her neck and her body jerked as pleasure shot down her spine from his hot kiss.

But her eyes were glued to Ravid as he tossed first one boot and then its twin aside. His eyes never left hers as he pulled his pants off. But hers fluttered as she slid them down his body. Fluid flowed down her passage as she looked at his swollen cock. There was another solid erection against her thigh and she shivered as she considered taking both of them into her body.

Keenan stiffened and lifted his head from her neck. He leaned over her shoulder and inhaled. Zeva shivered as she recognized that he could smell her arousal. It was a primitive thing that hit her in some dark corner of her mind. There was a part of her that wanted them both to know her body was wet for them. Just as her eyes enjoyed the sight of Ravid's swollen cock.

"Your scent drives me insane, *shihori*." Keenan caught her legs beneath her knees with one arm as he turned. The warrior was capturing her and a little zip of excitement hit her belly as Zeva recognized the pure strength of his embrace. Keenan's eyes were hard as he watched her face. "I have thought too many times about this moment."

Just as she had. Zeva trailed her fingers over his lips and grinned. They were still wet from her kiss and Keenan groaned as he turned towards the bed. It was a huge round one made to sleep all three of them. Her maiden's bed looked like a miniature compared to it. At that moment she couldn't help feeling like she was exactly where she wanted to be. Keenan let her down onto it gently as his lips lifted in a firm smile of satisfaction.

Doubt tried to wiggle into her thoughts but Zeva refused to notice it. She was far more interested in Ravid as he sat next to her. His dark eyes weren't probing into hers for a change. They feasted on her breasts, lingering over each globe as she held still for him.

"Do I meet with your approval, Ravid?" Astonishment covered his face as his eyes fastened onto hers. Zeva kept her face calm. She wasn't sure where she got the idea to tease a warrior like Ravid but the temptation tugged at her with irresistible appeal.

Zeva rolled back and caught her weight on her elbows. The posture thrust her breasts high and Ravid swallowed roughly as his dark eyes settled onto her nipples. "You should leave right now if I'm not acceptable. I certainly would not want you to make a mistake with an unacceptable female."

A low rumble of amusement came from Keenan as he tossed his coat aside. Zeva watched Ravid look at his partner with confusion written on his dark features, and she bit her lower lip to keep her giggle in her mouth.

Ravid still did not understand. His fingers were curled into the bedding as his knuckles turned white. Zeva caught the corner of a pillow and swung it at his head. The warrior jumped and landed on his feet, glaring at her. Zeva rolled onto her knees and propped her hands onto her hips because she knew it would make her breasts very obvious. Her lips twitched into a grin as Ravid fought to keep his eyes on her face and not her nipples.

"Are you quite certain, Ravid? Really, maybe I should just leave and save you the difficult task of rejecting me. My mother can take me home. Or maybe I could make do with just one mate, if Keenan isn't as picky as you."

Keenan was choking as Ravid rolled his eyes and caught the joke. Zeva's eyes sparkled with her teasing, making him stare at her in wonder again. This female could drive him insane but she wasn't afraid of him. It was a harsh fact of his life. Most people he encountered feared him and Keenan — that was one of the reasons their friendship was as powerful as it was.

"You truly are not afraid of me." Zeva felt an odd tug at her heart as Ravid cupped her face with his hand. His dark eyes were uncertain for a moment as he considered her. He stared at her with wonder and it humbled her slightly. Ravid certainly hadn't been someone she would have thought harbored insecurities.

"There are different kinds of fear, Ravid." The words came from her lips before she could stop them. It was a thought that tumbled out of her heart and her sense didn't engage fast enough to intercede. Zeva felt her composure shake as Ravid's dark eyes immediately captured hers. She shrugged as she lowered her body back onto her feet and crossed her arms across her breasts.

"Aye, there are." Ravid sat on the side of the bed. "I feared never to see you sitting in our bed." He crooked a single thick finger at her and tapped his lips as his eyes watched her reaction to his request. Her stomach twisted with nervousness but not fear. Strength might flow from both warriors but their honor was never in question to her.

She was safe in their bed from everything except her own body. Kissing Keenan had sent desire flowing down her body, and tasting Ravid was going to end every last notion of separation. Zeva raised her bottom off her feet and leaned

95

toward Ravid. She placed one hand on his shoulder to steady her body as she gently touched her mouth to his.

The taut muscle beneath her fingers shook as the warrior let her lead. His mouth opened with hers and moved at the same speed that she applied. A tiny moan of delight surfaced from her throat as Zeva let her tongue trace his lips. The little sound pushed Ravid beyond his limit and his hand caught her waist and pulled her forward.

Zeva moaned again as his mouth took hers. It was a hard kiss that matched the male holding her. His tongue stroked over her lips before demanding entry to her mouth. Keenan's scent joined Ravid's taste as he stroked her bare sides with his open hands. He teased the sides of her breasts as Ravid's tongue enticed hers to mingle.

She suddenly hated Keenan's pants. Her fingers moved over Ravid's chest, tracing the ridges of muscles, and her thighs rested against the harsh fabric of Keenan's pants. His erection burned into her thigh, taunting her with temptation. She suddenly felt empty, so empty she ached.

"The scent of your body will drive me insane, *ruthima*." Ravid growled the words against her mouth as he trailed his lips down her neck. His hand captured her hair and pulled her head back as she was bent over Keenan's arm. Her breasts were thrust high as Ravid teased one nipple with a soft kiss before sucking it into his mouth.

Her cry was harsh and Zeva wasn't even certain the sound came from her throat. It was too primal. Her eyes flew open as fire flowed from her nipple into her belly and she found Keenan's eyes locked with hers. He smiled at her pleasure as his fingers curled around her opposite breast, cupping the sensitive mound and raising the nipple up for Ravid.

Her hand landed on Keenan's chest as her eyes noticed that he had discarded his pants while her attention was on Ravid. Her eyes refused to stay locked with his as they moved over his chest to the hard cock thrusting up from his body.

Keenan's cock thrust straight out from his body. The head was ruby-red and the staff thick. Her belly twisted with need as she ran her eyes over him. She wouldn't be empty with that erection pressed deeply into her passage.

Keenan watched her face the entire time. Zeva's eyes flickered back to his and her pride surfaced at the uncertainly she caught drifting across his face. She might be a maiden but she was not fearful.

Moving her fingers, she ran them down his chest and over his abdomen. She traced the head of his cock and smiled at the feel of his weapon. His breath hissed as her hand closed around his staff and Zeva moved her grip down to the base and back up again. She shook off the pleasure of Ravid's sucking enough to recall her mother's instructions that had been given to her so many years ago. Alcandian females were never sent to their *triparh* without knowledge of a warrior's bed. Her mother's advice drifted past the pleasure as she eyed Keenan's erection.

Rolling over, she bent over Keenan's cock and let her tongue lick its head. A harsh grunt made her bold as she licked over that ruby head once more. The slit at its center held a single drop of fluid that she tasted before stroking his length with a firm grip.

"*Zeva*." Her name came from Keenan's chest like a plea as she opened her mouth and took his cock between her lips. She held the staff with her hand as she pulled her head back and tried to take more of his length into her mouth. Keenan's hand curled around her head as his breath hissed between his clenched teeth. His pleasure flowed into her mind as their mind-bridge gained strength. She moaned around his cock as she used her tongue to stroke the head.

Zeva pulled her mouth from Keenan as she turned her attention to Ravid. His dark eyes were focused on her and Keenan, and he watched as she stroked the length of Keenan's cock with her hand.

Zeva moved her hand up Keenan's cock and down once more as Ravid shot her a hungry look. She reached for his cock and curled her fingers around its hard length. Her breath came in little pants. The craving twisted in her passage, unwilling to be patient any longer. She clasped Ravid's cock as she stroked Keenan's once again. Ravid growled as she grasped his cock and she grinned at the sound. She was learning the tone of his growls. Now it was a deep sound of male appreciation as her fingers stroked and gripped his cock. His dark eyes closed to slits as his lips curled back to show her his clenched teeth.

"No maiden should be so bold, yet I do not lament it." Keenan caught her head as he whispered against her mouth. His lips pressed hers apart as his tongue thrust deeply into her mouth. Her passage twisted as it demanded the same thrust and fullness. In her hands their cocks throbbed with a promise she was eager for them to keep.

"Nay Zeva." Keenan lifted his head and pulled her hand from his cock. "Your body will be too tight." His eyes locked with hers as Ravid lifted her hand from his flesh as well.

Ravid laid a hand on her hip and rolled her backwards. His arm firmly pressed one of her thighs away from the other as Keenan pushed her shoulder down onto the mattress. Then she was on her back with the two looming over her. A tingle of fear swept through her as their shoulders rose above her with all that strength. She couldn't push it away and it mixed with her need, making her hips jerk with a motion born from pure instinct.

To submit or escape, Zeva wasn't sure. Ravid smoothed his large hand over her belly as he knelt on the floor next to the bed. Her eyes grew large as she watched him lower his dark eyes to the spread folds of her sex.

"You are so wet, *ruthima*." Her body glistened with her need and it drove him insane. Ravid slid his hand over her bare mons and into the soft folds of her sex. Her hips jerked and he laid a hand over one hip to hold her still. He needed to taste her. Drive her into pleasure so deeply that she would never leave his bed.

Spreading her lips with his thumb and finger he caught the little bud at the top of her folds with his mouth. She cried out as he did it and it fired his desire even more.

Zeva shook. Her body pulsed and shivered and control was nonexistent. Ravid's mouth was a flame that flickered over her tender sex and pulled on the very center of her need. He licked the little bundle of nerves and sucked it into his mouth as she writhed against the hold he pressed onto her hips.

"Let the pleasure take you, *shihori.*" Keenan cupped a breast and rolled the nipple between his fingers as she gasped. Everything was shattering under Ravid's mouth as the tip of his tongue flicked over her bud. He licked down the center of her sex to the opening of her passage and she cried as her body twisted up towards his mouth.

His tongue traveled back to the top of her sex and she cried at the loss. Her passage ached to be filled as he caught her bud once again and sucked on the little pleasure point. His hand suddenly appeared at her passage and one thick finger slowly entered her body in a smooth thrust.

Pleasure split her in two as she cried out. Ravid sucked her through the pulse of delight as he worked his finger in and out of her passage. A second finger joined his first one as he moved them both deeply into her body. When she collapsed back to the surface of the bed his face rose and his dark eyes probed hers. Male pride stared at her as he worked his fingers a few more times within her. "I have dreamed of doing that to you for too long, Zeva. I might spank your bottom for making me suffer so long."

"A good idea." Keenan pinched her nipple before slipping an arm under her waist and lifting her from the bed, his arms held her tightly to his chest and he rolled back onto the bed. He kept rolling until he pressed her back onto the bedding as he came down on top of her. His chest hair teased her nipples as her thighs parted to cradle his hips. The head of his cock stretched the opening of her body as he captured her head between his hands.

His body shook as he watched her eyes. Tension drew his face taut as he struggled to press his cock forward slowly. Her body burned but need tore at her harder than the discomfort. Her hips thrust upwards taking more of his cock as he cussed softly at her.

Keenan froze and Zeva burned for him to fill her. She reached for his head and lifted her hips higher. "Take me, Keenan. I need you inside me."

His breath hissed between clenched teeth as his eyes flickered with pure need. It was a primitive look that Zeva stared into because it was exactly what she craved. At that moment she didn't need society's rules and ceremonies. She wanted to mate.

Zeva curled her fingers around his biceps and purred at the thick muscle. She tilted her hips up as their thoughts mingled. "I am not fragile, Keenan."

Pride flashed through him and control dissipated. Zeva didn't lower her eyelashes, she stared into his eyes as her demand hung over him. Her passage was so wet his cock demanded to lodge its length in her body, need drove him to the edge of rational thought as her hips moved and he slid deeper into her.

Yet her words were correct. Offering Zeva comfort had never delivered her to his bed. She was a female who prized strength even so much so that the only males to possess her would be the ones who ran her to ground.

"Spread yourself wider, *shihori*."

Her fingernails bit into his skin as she complied. There was a hint of defiance flashing through her eyes and it made her even more desirable. There was a part of her that would never be completely conquered and it fired his need to pump his seed inside her.

She didn't cry out. Zeva clenched her teeth as Keenan's body surged into hers. Pain surrounded his cock as it split open her sheath and stretched it to accommodate him.

Keenan's fingers brushed the sides of her face as he dropped a soft kiss on her cheek. "Shhh…*shihori.*"

Zeva tossed her head and sucked in a deep breath. The pain burned away as she savored the feeling of being filled for the first time. The walls of her passage gripped his cock as her hips twitched with the need to move. She wanted more than just his cock inside her, she wanted to feel it thrust and move until her body received what it had been craving so much.

Zeva knew how mating was done, yet she never would have believed that it could feel so complete. She pulled her hand from one biceps and balled it into a fist. She hit Keenan's wide chest as he continued to torment her with nothing but that hard erection lodged deep inside her. "Must I ask Ravid to show me what is done next?"

"It would be my delight, *ruthima.*" Ravid's voice was dark. Zeva turned her head to look at him and stared at the raw desire blazing back at her. His fingers were fisted into the bedding as he watched Keenan begin to move between her thighs.

Zeva hadn't thought it possible for her desire to burn any hotter, but feeling Keenan moving inside her as she eyed Ravid's thick cock made her shudder. She reached for Ravid's erection as Keenan increased his pace and her hips lifted for him. Her fingers curled around his length as her body tumbled into a pleasure so acute she cried.

Keenan growled above her as he bucked and thrust his cock deeper into her. A hot spurt of seed hit her as his cock jerked and twitched inside her. Every muscle drew taut as the climax traveled through her and then it left her sagging to the surface of the bed with Ravid's hard cock still in her grip.

Keenan's eyes opened just inches above her own before he caught her mouth with his. He kissed her slowly as he slipped his tongue down the length of hers and back up again. "Aye, you have wasted far too many nights, Zeva. I confess I could curse the sun for rising tomorrow."

Keenan pulled his cock from her body and pushed his chest up. Cool night air rushed across her skin and she noticed that tiny beads of sweat covered her. Keenan lifted her from the bed before she'd even thought to close her spread thighs. He scooped her up in a tender hold as he took her across the chamber. The bed shimmered as Ravid stood up and the soiled bedding dissipated as new sheets appeared.

"I can walk, Keenan."

The warrior grinned at her as he stepped down into the bathing pool. "I enjoy knowing exactly where you are, Zeva." His eyes sparkled with enjoyment as he dipped her into the water like a child.

Zeva giggled as she rolled over and sank into the pool. Her body became weightless for a moment as she used her arms to push her head above the surface of the water. She pushed her hair back as water streamed down her back. Ravid stepped down into the water, his dark eyes still blazing with need.

She didn't just see it, she felt it. Emotions flowed between their minds as her body leapt with renewed desire. Setting her feet on the bottom of the pool, Zeva stood up to discover that this pool was much deeper than her own. The water came to her breast while it only covered Keenan's waist.

Keenan laid his arms on the sides of the pool as he watched her. Between them, Zeva once again felt surrounded but this time it was a perfect feeling of security. She wanted to be pressed between their bodies. Lying under Keenan had been pleasurable but being held in the center could be so much more.

Raising her arms out she reached for Ravid. The warrior snapped the instant her arms left the water in his direction. He captured her and pulled her against his body with arms that bound her to his length tightly. His mouth caught her just as firmly and the kiss was as hard as his cock.

Ravid thrust his tongue deeply into her mouth as his hands cupped her bottom. Her thighs opened to clasp his waist as he lifted her above his cock. The large head probed her body as he continued to kiss her. Zeva wrapped her hands around his neck as he thrust up into her body.

Her passage ached but pleasure still twisted her womb as he filled her. She tore her mouth from his as she gasped and struggled to pull more air into her lungs. Keenan's large body pressed into her back as Ravid began to thrust up into her with a hard pace that made her moan.

"When we are both inside you, you will scream with pleasure." Ravid's eyes almost glowed as he thrust hard into her with his words. Keenan smoothed a hand over her lower back and down to the spread checks of her bottom.

One finger teased her back opening as Ravid stopped deep inside her sheath. Keenan pressed his finger forward and Zeva moaned deeper. He pressed the digit up into her bottom before Ravid began to move again. Pleasure spiked into her as Keenan kept time with his brother and Zeva couldn't hold back the pleasure that wanted to break. She was finally full, so full her body wanted to climax over and over...as long as her mates kept moving into her. Keenan added a second finger and she came.

Climax broke, making her cry. Her hands twisted on Ravid's neck as his muscles corded and his seed shot up into her womb. Her passage clasped his cock and tried to milk every last drop of his climax.

Zeva lifted her eyes to see Ravid's nostrils flare. He growled low and deep and the sound made her confidence swell. Satisfaction filled his dark eyes and her mouth lifted into a grin in response. She had fed his need. Only her. Held between them she was the one female who could sate their desire, and in that moment it was the only thing she needed.

Ravid propped his head on an elbow hours later and stared at Zeva. She was restless in their bed. She shifted between their bodies because she was uncertain still. It wasn't a conscious decision she made, but it rubbed his pride.

"She will settle in time." Keenan's head appeared as he propped his head on an elbow as well. He stroked Zeva's hips with a slow hand and she shifted in her sleep rolling towards Ravid. Keenan sighed as he stroked her again.

Ravid felt her breath hit his chest and grinned. There were a thousand little things that he had never noticed about a female before. Taking his release with a widow had never taught him to enjoy the little moments like this when Zeva's scent made it possible to let his duties dissipate.

Right then there was only the three of them. Moonshine bathed Zeva's bare skin and he trailed his fingers over her, almost afraid she would disappear the second he touched her.

But she didn't and his fingers found her warm and smooth—the ideal of perfection simply because she was his mate. Even her stubborn independence was perfect. She would not be Zeva without it.

"Aye she will, brother."

She had to. He could not face this chamber without her. Keenan's eyes simmered in the dark over Zeva's body.

They could not face it without her!

# Chapter Six

🖎

Ravid's eyes snapped open. Something was wrong— different. The chamber was dark but silent. Dawn would arrive soon because the night was no longer black.

Zeva was missing.

A quick scan of the bed confirmed that only Keenan was still in it. Ravid rolled over the edge and onto his feet as he scanned the edges of the chamber for her. Amazement hit him as he absorbed the fact that she had managed to leave without waking him or Keenan.

It impressed him almost as much as it enraged him.

Memories of their night filled his head as his cock rose stiff and strong into the cool air. Hunger pounded through his blood as he reached for his uniform. Her scent clung to the bedding and even to his skin.

A smile lifted his lips as he lifted his boots from the floor. Zeva wanted to run? Well, she would have to accept the consequences of fleeing.

A hunter couldn't run prey to ground—unless it was running.

Keenan waited exactly one second after Ravid flung the doorway curtain aside before he rolled out of bed. Unlike his companion, his solution to Zeva's flight was more direct. His mate couldn't leave their bed if she had no place to go to.

A frown darkened his face as he moved through the curtain and down the steps.

\* \* \* \* \*

105

Tension couldn't hold on to her when she ran. Zeva pushed her body into motion, it demanded all of her concentration to keep her pace steady. An unbalanced foot meant disaster at this speed, and Zeva smiled as she lifted her knees higher to make her strides longer.

There was just the battle of will and flesh. Simple really, the body wanted to fold under the strain but she knew she would grow stronger if she held out against the nagging discomfort. Strength was built from dedication.

She cut across the female lands but kept the main house in sight. Jett had always scolded her for her running habit but she needed the illusion that she was alone.

Zeva didn't stop until the horizon turned pink. She dropped into a walk as her heart slowed down. Sweat soaked her hair and most of her clothing and she savored the proof that she had demanded the best from her body and gotten it.

A little laugh rumbled from her throat as she swung her arms in wide circles to keep the muscles from cooling too quickly. The privacy practically made her giddy like a little girl. Solitude wasn't what she craved, just the idea that she could be alone if she wanted to be. She had wanted to run and the freedom to grant her wish gave her peace.

The approaching day wasn't going to wait any longer though, and Zeva moved towards the boundary between the women's area and the warrior's one on the Judgment grounds. Her jacket was draped over a tree branch because she couldn't run in the long garment. As long as she was among females, a smaller top that supported her breasts called a *vertil* made running much easier.

Her coat wasn't where she'd left it. Instead it was flung over Ravid's wide shoulder as the warrior stood exactly one foot-length from the border. His face was drawn tight with anger and Zeva bit her lip as she tried to decide just why she shouldn't laugh at his temper.

She had gone running—big deal. The storm brewing in his dark eyes was a little extreme. But maybe the right word for it was possessiveness.

That idea banished her amusement. Tension flew up her neck muscles at the speed of light as Keenan appeared beside his partner with a deep frown on his face as well.

"Jett should have warned me that you are as foolish as a nearly weaned babe."

Zeva walked over the border with firm control lashed over her temper. She lifted one of her arms out for her coat. "And I would have enjoyed knowing that you are mean-tempered at sunrise before I spent the night with you. Thank goodness I arose before you."

Ravid growled, but she was getting used to the sound. It just fit him and Zeva dropped her arm to her side as she recognized that he was not going to give her anything she wanted, even her coat. "Very well, Ravid, I am not ashamed of my body and will be quite content to walk back across warrior land in my *vertil*."

Zeva turned away and did just that. Keenan scooped her off her feet before she passed the silent warrior. A little woof was the only sound she made as his arm clamped around her midsection and pulled her off the ground. Zeva ground her teeth together because Keenan swung her up and onto his shoulder. Her temper ignited as he slapped her bottom.

Zeva took her turn to growl before she erupted upwards. Keenan tried to clasp her in his arms but she twisted and fell to the ground with a hard smack. She slapped away the hands that tried to help her up, as she forced her feet under her. Her hip shrieked with pain where she'd impacted and her leg muscles wobbled, threatening to collapse instead of hold her up. "You will not haul me about like a prize! I refuse!"

"You enjoy the slide of that word on your lips far too much, Zeva." Keenan's voice was too low. Zeva knew the sign of his temper now and she glared at him as she shook her leg.

His frown darkened as he watched the telltale sign of pain. Guilt also shone from his eyes as he looked at the leg she was favoring. "You should trust me, Zeva. I would not have dropped you if you stayed still."

"I will not be treated like a child, Keenan."

"Then stop acting like one." Ravid was moving slowly around her. Caging her between Keenan and himself. He was also placing himself in front of the border to the female section. Zeva looked from one to the other and groaned as her body tingled with awareness. She fought for control over her temper as she tried to find some shred of logic to their anger. The moments spent cuddled between their two bodies lingered in her thoughts as she looked at the harsh disapproval being aimed at her now. Her desire to quarrel was strangling as her body clamored for another night in their bed.

"I run every morning. Why are you two so angered by that? You know my body is fit." Zeva cast a harassed look at Ravid. "And stop maneuvering me between you. I walked over that border willingly enough. It's insulting that you feel the need to restrain me like some deviant."

Ravid felt his face flush and stopped in his tracks. He was working on instinct, cornering Zeva out of pure desire to secure her in his bed. Yet she held a good point. It was far past time they learned to communicate. Zeva took a deep breath before she lifted her arm again. "Are you willing to give me my jacket back?"

Her effort wasn't lost on either warrior. Keenan felt a wave of shame hit him because his control should never have allowed his temper to take over. It was an unacceptable lapse that made him struggle against the wave of lust her *vertil* inspired. Yet there was good reason he had become angry at her disappearance.

"Zeva, you must not leave our chamber without us until we bind." Her frown returned as she shrugged into her coat. "It is not safe for you to return to Sinlar female grounds. You need to remain on Judgment grounds."

"Aye. The warrior grounds." Ravid forced his body to move closer to Keenan's. Zeva watched the tight line of his lips as he moved in spite of his wishes. It was such a small thing but the gesture was truly appreciated because it felt like trust.

Zeva shook her head. Trust? She did not need to feel trusted by them. That emotion could lead to so many other…deeper ones. But the brain and the heart didn't always agree and she felt her lips twitching up as Keenan nodded approval at his companion.

"I can handle my own safety while jogging on the women's grounds. I have never had reason to fear Sinlar ground and I am not going to begin. It is my home." Sinlar was her family group. The Judgment grounds lay between four separate Alcandian clans. Warriors like Ravid and Keenan cast off their own family identity when they put on the maroon coats of their enforcement duty.

"It *was* your home, Zeva." Keenan stated the words in a hard tone that made her stare at him. He often appeared as the gentler member of their team but Zeva was learning that that was nothing but a clever ploy that allowed him to strike exactly when he wanted to. His prey never saw the predator until it was too late. Right then his eyes were trained on hers, just waiting for her to deny his claim that her home was now in his chamber.

She could not deny the binding fever, it burned through her and across the morning air. She could feel the two warriors merging with her emotions. Nothing her logic wanted would change that fact. It was genetically encoded into her flesh.

"If binding with you means becoming a frightened little bird, I will discover a way to live with frustration."

She had even stayed on Judgment female grounds just to not rub their pride. But it looked like her effort was completely lost. That didn't raise her temper, instead a wave a lament crossed her. Maybe if there was some place in the middle that the three of them could meet… Zeva shook off the idea. Ravid and Keenan didn't look like negotiation was a word present in their vocabulary.

"A fool—" Keenan cleared his throat and Ravid snapped his lips closed on the word. Ravid considered her with dark eyes before he closed his fingers into a fist. "Once you wear our bracelet we can protect you, Zeva. Then you may run on the female grounds. Judgment female grounds. You need only stay in our home until our binding ceremony. We should have explained that to you last evening."

Ravid's voice shook with the effort he used to hold his temper in. Zeva battled against her own because she wanted to scream at them in return. She would not be shackled like a prisoner!

Not ever again.

But she was sorry. Both warriors looked at her with eyes that denied her any discussion on the topic. They intended their will to be obeyed.

"I have classes to teach." Zeva turned to leave but Ravid caught her arm in a hard grip.

"Release me, Ravid! My life is mine for the next two risings." Anger flared in his eyes but Zeva tore her arm from his grip and left. Her emotions spun out of control. She didn't want to fight with them but couldn't swallow the dictates that would take away the life that she had just regained.

Tears spilled down her cheeks and it made her even madder. She did not cry! Zeva wiped her hand across her face and stared at the shiny smears of water on her palm.

Curse and rot it all! Only Keenan and Ravid could make her so emotional. The reason was so clear that it made another round of tears drop from her eyes. They touched her in a place that no one had ever reached.

Her heart.

\* \* \* \* \*

"Zeva, are you all right?" Her sister-in-law knew otherwise but Jessica hovered in the doorway and crossed her arms across her chest as she eyed Zeva.

"Warriors are a pain, but you learn to appreciate the advantages of having them around sometimes." Jessica grinned and Zeva propped her hands onto her hips.

Jessica was a human Dylan had discovered on Earth. She was also Cole Somerton's sister. Right at that moment, Jessica looked as Alcandian as Zeva. Twice a week she worked in Zeva's studio's office. Teaching defense arts was something Zeva was very good at. Writing the contracts that kept her studio doors open was another matter.

So, she had hit Jessica up for help even before the human girl had decided to bind with her brother. She and Jessica shared a bond that went so much deeper than work. It was Jessica who York had been trying to keep on Earth when the humans destroyed the Alcandian gate.

"Advantages? Well, maybe." Zeva grinned at Jessica. Sharing a chamber with Ravid and Keenan had gone far beyond the word advantage. It was pleasure incarnate. Something women tried to explain to maidens but never could truly communicate.

Her body still pulsed with little ripples of excitement. Her passage was sore but not painful. The little ache only reminded her of how she felt when the two warriors were inside her.

Zeva shook her head and tried to remember what she and Jessica were talking about. Jessica laughed and rubbed her growing stomach. Zeva let her eyes drop to the coming addition to her family. "You didn't wait very long."

Jessica sighed and shrugged. "No, Sandor is Jett's son and even though Dylan loves him, I can see that he wants a child too." Jessica considered Zeva with a thoughtful look. "I guess you'll have to decide how long to wait yourself before long."

Would she? It both terrified and thrilled her. Both Ravid and Keenan would be expected to consider any child of her body as their offspring but it wasn't at all uncommon for females to do exactly what Jessica was. Make certain that each warrior had a child.

It was even possible that her belly was right at that moment cradling a new life. A silly smile threatened to break out on her face and Zeva bit her lip to keep her face smooth. The temptation that had been nagging her all day, gained amazing volume as she looked at Jessica's rounded belly.

She had two more nights before the binding ceremony. During that time, she was free to indulge her body. It was expected that she would have sex with Ravid and Keenan — in fact, it was encouraged. That was the Alcandian way of discovering if you could build a life together.

Jessica laughed. "Oh Zeva, you need to go home." Her sister-in-law giggled again and Zeva felt her jaw drop open.

"I seem to remember you being rather set against binding."

Jessica's smile grew brighter. "Yes, and I must admit that I enjoyed having my mind changed."

Zeva glared at Jessica and her happiness. Jessica laughed because she had rebelled against her claiming quite loudly.

"Zeva, you need to take all that frustration out on your mates. The three of you will never work anything out while you hide here." Jessica flung her hand up into the air and half turned towards the door. "You know Keenan once told me to ask for what I wanted from my mates. He had a very good point. You can't get what you want out of a relationship if you don't ask for it."

Jessica disappeared, leaving Zeva looking at the setting sun. Her instruction staff was teaching class and had looked at her in wonder when she had shown up for work today. They didn't need her now. Guilt sailed right into her thoughts as she looked at the work she'd accomplished so little of.

She was hiding. Her teeth crushed against each other as she faced her own cowardice. It was her pride that held her back. Her body would delightfully fling itself into the arms of the two warriors who had proven how well they could feed her desires.

It was really rather ironic. How did you live in a body and not know the needs that drove it? Sure, she had often been curious about mating, how it might feel and what exactly climax did to a woman. Her lips still tingled today as her memory replayed Keenan's kiss.

Heat flowed over her skin, awakening each little nerve. Deep inside her passage she ached for that completion that Ravid had produced with his harder body. Her nipples drew tighter but they had never completely flattened out. Her body was twisting and pulsing with the desire to return to Ravid and Keenan. Maybe her brain had lots of reasons why she should force a separation but it wasn't enough to banish the wave of need. It rose from places on her skin that she hadn't considered very important. Like her hip. The way Keenan stroked his large hand over her thigh sent fluid rushing into her passage.

It also sent two little tears into her eyes. The touch was more than lust-driven. Even Ravid with his harder edges, tempered his touch to something that glided over her body, making her heart swell.

Ask them?

She just might do that. Her body gave a halfhearted lament and she smiled. Talking with Ravid and Keenan tended to lead to sleep with frustration, but if Jessica could find peace with the warriors who had abducted her from Earth and even learn to love them…

It just might be possible to hold a civil conversation with her intended mates.

*Maybe.*

\* \* \* \* \*

Jessica finished her last task and grinned at the studio office. It was neat and organized...at least until she left it would be!

Her baby kicked and she smoothed a hand over her belly. The windows rattled making her frown. She was alone in the studio, last class ending a half hour ago. Standing up, she looked across the mat but didn't see anyone. A tingle ran down her neck as she hesitated in the office doorway. It might be the wind but the windows always rattled that way when one of the doors opened. She would have seen anyone coming in through the front door but the back one was hidden by the changing rooms.

A hand landed on the front door and Jessica jumped. Jett aimed a puzzled look at her as she passed her hand over the lock control.

"What troubles you?" Jett's hand landed on her swollen belly as he claimed a kiss from her mouth.

"Um...nothing." Just her imagination. Jessica looked at the control panel and it showed both doors closed. It was nothing.

Craddock wanted to laugh. He did enjoy beating his opponent. The studio security system didn't even chirp as he opened the back door of the building. He pulled free the small circuit reroute he'd stuck into the door sensor before he left. A smirk lifted his lips as he looked around before moving off into the cover of some nearby foliage. Females would never be able to outsmart a warrior. He would go anywhere he liked and take whatever he wanted.

But Zeva wasn't in the studio. Craddock frowned as he moved across Sinlar land. The human didn't interest him. Yet the day was not a total loss. Knowing your prey was the best way to hunt. Zeva's studio was rich with information and ways to lure her away from Ravid and Keenan.

\* \* \* \* \*

"Glaring at the door will not bring her here sooner, Ravid." Amin was cheerful as always. Ravid grimaced and his sister-in-law smiled wide enough to display her teeth. She ended the expression with a loud kiss that she blew across the table at him. Keenan laughed at her.

"Amin, you must have been born giggling instead of wailing."

Amin shrugged and had to catch her coat before one side slid off her thin shoulder. Ravid frowned as he reached for his arm control and pressed a command into the communications link. A platter of fruit appeared on the table and he pushed it gently towards Amin. The first frown he'd seen on her face that day was his reward.

"Worry about your own mate, Ravid. I am fine."

Keenan huffed under his breath and Ravid gave the platter another little shove. "You are wasting away."

"What are a few pounds?" Amin toyed with a purple berry. "There aren't any extra pounds on Zeva. Are you planning on plumping her up?"

Keenan tossed a piece of fruit into his mouth before shaking his head. "Leaving her studio will affect her body but she can not continue spending her days off the Judgment grounds."

Amin's eyebrows rose as she looked at Ravid for his opinion. The darker warrior sighed. "Helmut and Craddock are still alive." Ravid felt his temper burn. It was a slow seep of anger that moved through him any time he thought about the deviants who had struck his brother down. There would be justice for the fallen Judgment officials someday. He and Keenan would not rest until it happened. "Zeva will have to spend her time within this hall once we bind. I wish it were within our control to insist she begin doing that now."

A soft hiss hit his ears and he turned. Zeva stood there with her fingers curled into fists as temper brightened her cheeks. Ravid stood up as he watched her teeth bite into her lower lip as she tried to keep her mouth silent. More anger poured through his brain as he watched her battle the urge to yell at him. Confining Zeva to protected Judgment grounds gave him no joy. Being forced to do it because of deviants enraged him.

Yet he would do what was needed to ensure her safety.

Keenan stepped forward with a heavy look on his face. "Best we retire now."

Zeva looked at him before nodding her head. "Aye."

Their chamber was set once again with little details that tempted her to melt. Tonight there were bowls of dried spices set out. The air was rich with delicious scents. Water flowed down a wall filling the air with its soothing sound and Zeva wanted to scream at fate. They held the right to demand her body in their bed, yet they planned her seduction.

"We need to speak, Zeva." Keenan used his soothing voice as Ravid stood back to allow him to take the lead. Zeva watched the ultrasmooth way they worked together. It was polished to perfection.

Just as it had been last night when they loved her body.

Zeva shook her head. She could not bend so completely to their will. Keenan watched her with his light-colored eyes and she lifted her chin to stare back at him. "Aye, we do if you think I will give up my studio."

"It is not on Judgment grounds, Zeva. You are unsafe there. Today was endless for us." Keenan reached for her shoulder and she moved from his reach. His eyes flashed at her, confusing her, until Ravid captured her wrist and stroked the skin under her wrist with his thumb. Triumph flashed across his eyes and her body shivered with a little ripple of pleasure. Her passage filled with hunger as Ravid held firmly onto her.

"Stop it, Ravid! I cannot think when you touch me." The words left her mouth once more before she thought about them. Ravid's mouth twitched up at the corners into a huge grin and Zeva groaned. "Either we are talking or not. But I cannot bind myself to warriors who do not accept me as I am."

Ravid growled at her. It was a harsh sound that made her step back from him. He snapped her forward with his grip on her wrist and clamped her body against his. "You will bind with me, Zeva! If I must wring the words from your body."

Dark promise lit his eyes making her jerk against his embrace. There was no hope of release. His body was twice the size of hers, surrounding her with hard muscle created by nature to help ensure the conception of the next generation.

Ravid could hold her down but that wasn't what frightened her the most. It was the simmering of desire blazing in his eyes that promised her he would do exactly what he said he would.

Use her body against her will.

"Ravid—" His mouth thrust the rest of her words back into her throat. He demanded entry to her mouth as his hand caught the back of her head, tilting her neck back as he thrust his tongue deeply into her mouth.

Her nipples twisted into little buttons against his chest, almost like they were stabbing into the hard muscle as a form of communication. Ravid's tongue thrust and stroked hers, making her clit clamor for the same treatment. She wanted so many things in that moment. Both touch and kiss and she wanted it to be as hard as the warrior holding her against him.

Her hand moved over his chest as Keenan joined their embrace. His hard body moved along her back making a contented purr rise from her throat. His lips found her shoulder and gently bit her. Fluid coated the walls of her passage as his large hands stroked over the cheeks of her bottom. What had they promised her?

*Both of them.*

Zeva shook as Keenan reached for the drawstring of her pants. Ravid's mouth lifted from hers as his dark eyes blazed into hers. His breath hit her wet lips sending another wave of sensation over them. Her hands tried to slide under his coat as frustration made her angry.

Ravid smiled slightly. Just a little rise at the corners of his mouth but the expression didn't reach his eyes. Pure determination still blazed there as he stepped away from her. Keenan bound her to his body with his thick arms, immobilizing her.

"I like the look of you in my brother's arms, Zeva." Ravid opened his coat and pulled it down his arms. Each muscle was sharply defined as he reached for the waistband of his pants. "Yet your lips are swollen from my kiss and that is even more to my liking."

Keenan growled against her neck as his teeth nipped the tender skin. Ravid watched his companion as he stepped out of his pants and tossed them over a chair. Her eyes dropped to his cock and her breath caught in her throat.

He was hard and swollen. Zeva shivered as Keenan's erection pressed into her back. Her sheath ached to hold them. The sharply defined muscles coating Ravid's bare form promised her a hard ride. No sweet seduction but the hard overpowering that she craved.

Maybe she had always needed to be conquered. Zeva battled against the primitive thought but it sent a wave of excitement through her too. It shook her confidence to find an idea like that hidden deep inside her but at the moment she didn't want to ponder her findings.

She wiggled in Keenan's embrace, not frantically, just a slow squirm that pressed against Keenan's erection and his breath hissed next to her ear. A smile lifted her lips but she had forgotten that Ravid watched her face. The warrior shook his head as his fingers curled around her chin to lift it to his eyes as he stepped closer.

"Maybe you do not understand yourself, Zeva." His eyes considered her before his head dipped to her neck and he inhaled her scent. More fluid coated the walls of her passage because her body wanted him to know she was wet and ready for his possession. His eyelids lifted to display pure desire burning in his eyes. "Yet, possibly you understand far more than I think you do."

Confidence brightened her eyes and Ravid groaned. He might want to indulge in the idea of capture but Zeva just might rise to meet his challenge. His nostrils flared slightly as his blood surged through his veins. His cock jerked as he savored the hot scent of her arousal.

"Come here." It was an order and Zeva considered refusing. Her body twisted with the need to be next to Ravid's bare skin. Keenan's hands pulled her pants down her legs and she sighed as the night air brushed her skin. She stepped out of her pants and forward towards Ravid.

Zeva stopped short of the embrace. She laid her hands on his chest and traced the muscles coating his chest. She touched him with just her fingertips, gliding the sensitive digits over each millimeter of warm male skin. She moved her hands down his abdomen until she slipped her fingers around his cock.

The organ jerked in her hand making her shift her thighs apart. Her passage burned for the hard length and she slipped to her knees as she caught the head between her lips.

Ravid cussed and she took his cock deeper into her mouth. Power surged through her as she sucked him deeper and used her tongue to rub the spot under the swollen head. A hand caught her head and twisted her hair but Zeva cupped the sac holding his seed and licked around his cock head again. She pushed her closed hand down the length as she sucked and Ravid's hips thrust towards her.

It was instinct and she increased her efforts. There would always be this struggle between them. The need to be the one driving the other to the edge of insanity. Deep in her brain she craved the hot spurt of his seed hitting her tongue, just to satisfy some primitive craving to push this male past his control. She wanted to wring a cry of pleasure from him and be in control as he shattered with climax.

Their minds mingled as she licked and stroked his cock. His breath hissed between clenched teeth as Zeva took more length into her mouth. The hand on her hair pulled as his hips jerked. Pleasure flowed between their link as his seed hit her mouth. Zeva savored the moment as Ravid labored to catch his breath and her hand stroked his cock.

She didn't rise from her knees. Instead she turned and caught Keenan's newly bared cock with her hands and applied her lips to its swollen head. The warrior gasped and stepped back. Zeva followed and sucked his cock back into her mouth.

"Zeva, you will reduce me to my tender years." Keenan groaned low as she refused to leave his cock. Her lips drove him insane as her little tongue flickered over his cock. Climax hadn't come so quickly since he was newly introduced to a woman's charms. With Zeva, a few short moments in her mouth and his seed strained against his control to keep it from shooting into her.

Yet there was not a need to resist. Keenan stroked the head of his mate and let pleasure crest over his control. Zeva. His. It was perfection after longing for it for too many years. The fact that she wanted to bring him to climax first just made it even more incredible. "You may bend me to your whim any time, Zeva."

Zeva stood up and watched Ravid as he smiled at her. It still wasn't a friendly expression. A shiver raced down her spine as he cupped one of her breasts and pressed his thumb over her nipple. Tight control covered his face as he watched her and gently squeezed her breast. Ravid leaned down and finished Keenan's comment. "As long as you are willing to be bent to my will in return."

A little moan escaped her lips. It was pure instinct. She could smell how much he wanted her, still taste it and the desire flowed between their minds as Keenan's body pressed into her back. Ravid stroked his hand across her chest to her other breast before he bent and sucked her nipple into his mouth.

Fire shot down her body. Her belly twisted with an ache so hard it hurt. She needed him inside her. She craved his cock thrusting deeply into her passage to fill it. The bud at the top of her sex throbbed with a demand to be sucked between his lips just like her nipple was. Zeva reached for his head and twisted her fingers in his hair as her back arched to offer her nipple up to his mouth.

"You may not come yet, Zeva." Keenan's voice was low and hard. His hands moved over her hips as he pulled her off her feet. She whimpered as Ravid released her nipple and Keenan took her away from his companion. She wanted them both!

"You will have us, *ruthima*, yet at our demand." Keenan laid her on the bed but only her torso. He turned her facedown and let her legs hang over the edge. His hand stroked her bottom before Ravid joined them. "Spread your legs."

Zeva moaned again at the order. So much pleasure could be hers if she obeyed. A little twist of fear joined her need as she parted her thighs and slipped her feet across the tile floor. Keenan leaned over her, leaving her to guess what Ravid was intending to do. A hundred little maidens' whispers crossed her brain. Unbound females talked about warriors' bedchambers and the delights certain games could produce.

Would they spank her? Ravid had suggested it just last night. Zeva tried to lift her body off the bed but Keenan held her flat to the bed surface. He nuzzled her ear before she felt a hand on her bottom once again.

"Your bottom is too tight for a cock, *shihori*." Keenan licked her ear before he finished. "So it needs to be stretched before we can enjoy you at the same time."

She gasped and Keenan made a soft soothing sound against her ear. His body pressed her down as Ravid pulled her bottom apart. She shivered but it was born of excitement. Ravid touched her back entrance with a smooth liquid and her hips jerked towards his hand. He mumbled with deep approval before more of that lubricant was applied to her bottom.

They would use a plug on her. Zeva knew what one looked like because her mother had bought her one. It wasn't uncommon for an Alcandian female to stretch her bottom before taking that first step towards intimacy with a warrior. She just hadn't had time to think about using the little silver anal plug that Paneil had given her. Since her return from Earth everything had moved too quickly for her to remember little details like her anal plug.

Ravid pressed the tip of one against her bottom and she gasped. He had warmed it somehow and the tip pressed forward through the lubricant that he'd coated her bottom with. Keenan turned to watch as her back entrance stretched wider and wider as Ravid pushed it further into her body.

Zeva gasped as the pressure bordered on pain. Ravid held the plug in place as his hand stroked over her bottom. He pulled the plug out and then pressed it forward again. Pleasure replaced discomfort as he worked the toy in and out, going a little further with each thrust.

"Aye Zeva, your bottom was made to be filled." Ravid's voice was almost harsh, and then he pressed the plug deeply into her. It stretched her bottom until it smarted but it also pressed the walls of her passage together making her squirm with need.

"I can smell your need." Ravid stroked her bottom again before Keenan lifted her and turned her onto her back. That little twist of fear came back as she found her body in the center of the bed with both warriors looming over her. She was helpless against their greater strength. But she savored it too. It was more than the iron muscles. Their clash of wills made them more attractive to her. Warriors were not meant to be controlled by a female. Zeva knew she would have rejected them if they were too compliant.

Maybe they sought her out for the same reason.

Keenan's hands cupped a breast as the warrior leaned forward to suck its nipple. Zeva muttered with delight as his tongue worried her nipple. Her eyes flew open as Ravid pressed her thighs apart. His eyes were focused on her open sex. Raw possession glittered from the dark orbs before they flickered up to hold hers for a moment. "You may not like the word, Zeva, but when you cry out, it will be my tongue that is mastering your sweet body."

His hands held her thighs wide as her hips jerked. Her pride didn't have a chance of breaking his hold on her. The bud at the top of her sex pounded in time with her heart. It demanded she submit so that release could be hers.

But Ravid wouldn't deny her that even if she forced the words past her lips. His eyes glittered with the desire to bring her to climax. His eyes moved back to the spread folds of her body before he leaned forward to suck that little bud into his mouth.

Her head arched back as pleasure ripped into her belly. Words lost their value as Ravid sucked and licked her clit. Keenan moved to her other breast and her hands curled into the bedding. There was only need and heat. Waves of flames that began under each warrior's tongue and shot into her core. Her hips jerked with the need to lift. She wanted to be filled, not just sucked. Nothing mattered but that craving.

"Fill me, Ravid!"

Her voice was sultry and Zeva almost didn't recognize it. The woman the world saw wasn't there in that chamber. In her place was a female burning with heat. She wanted to mate.

Ravid felt his body shake, and groaned. He ran his tongue down her sex to the entrance of her passage and denied his cock the dark opening to his mate. He was going to pleasure her with his mouth and even his hands before plunging his cock into her. Both desires tore at him, one born from his will and the other from his flesh. Ravid moved back up to her clit and thrust a finger into her body as he sucked her.

A harsh cry was his reward as her hips lifted and her passage greedily tried to milk his finger. Her head thrashed on the bed as he thrust his finger in time with the jerks from her hips.

"I enjoy bringing you to pleasure as much as you do us, Zeva." Ravid thrust his finger deeply into her body again as her eyelids lifted to display her dark eyes to him. "The plug has made your body so tight, my cock nearly drives me mad with the idea of getting inside you."

A low rumble of agreement came from Keenan's chest as he left her nipple and looked down her body to where Ravid moved that single finger in and out of her. Ravid moved and knelt between her thighs. Up on his haunches, he pulled her bottom from the bed as his cock thrust forward between them. Keenan watched as his companion fit the head of his cock against the entrance of her body and slowly pushed the swollen organ into her. Zeva was caught between both warriors, the one who thrust into her and the one who watched.

Keenan cupped her breast as Ravid pulled her onto his cock. Her bottom still didn't touch the bed, just her shoulders. Ravid's hands gripped her hips and pulled her onto his cock until he stretched her with it and then he pulled his hips back to leave her passage screaming for the next thrust.

"Ah Zeva, your body was made for mine." Ravid snarled the words softly as he pulled her onto his cock again. He lingered inside her as he raised his eyes to her. "The only thing better will be when we both take you."

Zeva whimpered at the idea. Her body was so full with the plug in her bottom. Ravid pushed her off his cock and then pulled her back. This time he didn't stop inside her passage. His hands held her lower body up and worked it on and off his cock. Her head moved from side to side but she was powerless to move her hips. Ravid worked them at his speed as she sobbed and cried out with a climax that ripped into her womb.

Ravid grunted harsh approval a second before he slammed his cock deeply into her. His cock jerked and pumped his seed deeply into her. His fingers dug into her hips as he held her impaled on his cock until the last of his seed was deep inside her.

His dark eyes snapped open and sought hers. Concern raced through them as he gently let her bottom rest back on the bed. His warm body covered hers as he stroked the sides of her face. "Did I hurt you?"

Zeva laughed at his question. Ravid watched a sparkle cross her eyes as her hands traced his biceps. Sweat beaded in her hair as he stroked her face again. Contentment landed on his shoulders as he watched her lips lift in a small smile. Ravid rolled onto his back and took Zeva with him. She landed against his chest and his body enjoyed the weight. Being in contact with her fed his longings. Seeing her wasn't enough, mating with her wasn't enough, he craved the scent of her pleasure and the weight of her satisfied body on his for true contentment.

The plug felt small now. Zeva felt Keenan's hands stroke her bottom as Ravid's heart beat beneath her hands. Hunger still flowed from Keenan's mind and it sparked a response from her body.

Pushing up off Ravid, she turned to her other warrior. Keenan watched her with hungry eyes as she pushed back onto her feet and swung one thigh over his hip. She pushed his chest with one hand as one of his eyebrows rose.

"Lie down, Keenan." The warrior did it reluctantly. Zeva moved over his body and leaned down to kiss him. She teased his mouth with the tip of her tongue before raising her hips above his cock. He was still hard and her wet body opened for him easily. Zeva lowered her bottom and moaned as she was once again filled completely.

A loud smack hit her bottom making her gasp. Keenan smiled and caught her hips before she rose off his cock. Another blow landed on her bottom as Ravid bit her shoulder. Keenan's grin grew larger as his hands lifted her up and then let her body weight push her back onto his cock. "I believe I could become quite fond of letting you ride me, Zeva." His hands left her hips to cup her breasts. "Aye, very fond."

Keenan pinched her nipples right before Ravid smacked her bottom again. "Ride him, *ruthima*. Do you need encouragement?" Two more smacks hit her bottom as Zeva lifted her body up and let gravity send her back onto Keenan's cock.

Keenan's pinches on her nipple joined the sharp sting of Ravid's spanking, making her twist on the hard cock stretching her body. The plug made it so tight she had to use her legs to push up off Keenan. Ravid smacked her bottom again, making her cry. Climax wouldn't come easily though. Pleasure flowed from her nipples to her bottom as she rose up and pressed down.

"You are so wet." Keenan's voice was strained as his neck muscles drew taut. His hand curled around her hips a second before his body surged off the bed. He rolled her over as he came down and thrust hard between her thighs. His fingers caught her wrists and stretched her hands across the bed as his hips thrust hard into her body.

"Take me, Zeva! I want your passage to milk my cock!" His body jerked but he held off his climax as his eyes stared into hers. His pleasure flowed through their mind link, dragging her body with his into pleasure. It tore across from his mind into hers as his hips drove his cock deeply into her.

Her body was one single current of delight. Zeva couldn't tell the difference between her flesh and Keenan's or Ravid's. Their bodies just mingled and curved around each other's so completely. Her mind was too tired to care. They carried her to the bathing pool and smoothed soap over her skin, cleaning the sweat off her. Keenan even cleaned the folds of her sex with a gentle hand before he pulled the anal plug from her bottom. The warm water lured her even further from thoughts and reasons and anything that meant leaving their embrace.

Keenan enjoyed carrying Zeva. Truthfully, he had never enjoyed weakness in any female but holding her half-slumbering body against his chest was completely satisfying. His lips tightened into a thin line as he looked at the hand she let rest against his chest. She was at peace in his embrace and he was going to have to change that.

As he placed her on the bed, her eyes opened when she tried to move up to lay her head on a pillow. Keenan held her waist and sat her up. "We need to talk, Zeva."

The tone of his voice sliced through Zeva's desire to sleep. She sat back on her knees and found Ravid watching her with serious eyes. In a split second, while her eyes had been closed, both males had transformed into Judgment officials. Firm resolve covered their faces as Ravid sat on the opposite side of the bed.

"I meant to tell you before we wore you out." Keenan frowned as Zeva moved back on her knees ending all contact with his body. Whatever was on his mind, Zeva got the idea that she wasn't going to like it. Casting her eyes sideways, she considered Ravid. His face was dark with fury as he watched her. His words sliced through the dark room as he clamped a hard hand around her wrist.

"You saw Amin at the table tonight. She was my sister-in-law, bound to my brother."

"Was?" Since Amin still had her hair and was welcome by Ravid, there was only one other thing that would have ended her union. The anger blazing from Ravid's eyes made her temper stir but this time it joined his rage.

127

Ravid nodded and his thumb slipped under her wrist to stroke the skin. The touch was an odd addition to the tension flowing from Ravid's emotions. It was a tiny tender gesture that made it impossible to separate her trust of the hour past from this current moment of pure Judgment authority. Somehow, the warrior didn't want to press his will onto her carelessly. The little caress was a soothing offer in the face of something that he knew she was not going to like. "Chandler was a Judgment official. He was struck down by a deviant who still breathes."

Keenan caught her chin and turned her eyes to his. "Helmut and Craddock are *thydit*, yet outlawed and move through any land they can survive on. You must not expose yourself to their sight, Zeva. They would not kill you."

Horror flashed through her brain because Zeva understood what Keenan meant. There was a reason warriors like Ravid and Keenan roamed Alcandar. They rid the planet of filth.

Like this Helmut and Craddock. Males like that were the same as mad animals. They would kill and destroy at whim until someone put them down. If they would not kill her, they would use her body. If Keenan knew they would not kill her, then she would not be the first female the deviants had abused.

It was a high crime on Alcandar. Among a race that had too few females, mating was governed by strict laws and tradition. A woman only had to submit to warriors who proved she was attracted to them. Her own attraction was forcing her will to bend. Ravid and Keenan were not allowed to hurt her. Even their chamber had only a half wall that overlooked the main warrior eating hall below stairs. A thick curtain could be drawn for privacy but all upper chambers were constructed in such a manner.

The reason was simple. Any cries from a female would be heard. A slight blush stained her cheeks because the last hour had truly been witnessed by some of Ravid's and Keenan's comrades.

"I am sorry to hear of your mother's loss." Zeva was, too. She stood up as emotion tried to flood her eyes with tears. She needed to move because the walls were collapsing in on her. She might not like it but she wasn't foolish enough to refuse to heed Ravid's warning. She had always known that becoming involved with Judgment officials meant sharing their remote life.

She walked to the window seat and looked out. Light spilled from other houses and from walkways. The Judgment grounds were neat and well groomed. As a home, she would not want for anything but freedom.

Ravid's arms closed around her. His embrace stopped just short of pain as he squeezed her against his chest. His chin rested on top of her head as he inhaled her scent. "Fate makes many choices we do not like, Zeva."

From Ravid, it was almost an apology. Two tears dripped down her cheeks as her hands landed on his forearms. It just felt so right in his arms! The rest of her brain was screaming and struggling but her heart was so full she just wanted to close her eyes and float into the comfort of that embrace.

A little sigh escaped her lips as Zeva let her head rest against his chest. The night air was cool and her nipples tightened with the chill. Ravid's arms moved as he lifted her from her feet. She glared at him as he carried her towards Keenan and their bed. "I walk very well."

Keenan reached for her as Ravid settled her between them. Both warriors moved closer until she was pressed between them. Their legs tangled as she turned on her side. Her back lay against Ravid and her hands rested on Keenan. Ravid never answered her and maybe she didn't need him to. There was still that part of her that enjoyed being captured. Apparently, Ravid enjoy that little struggle too. Placing her in his bed fed some male need that wouldn't enjoy her walking across the floor quite as much. Who knew for certain?

Zeva let her eyes slip shut as the scent of her warriors filled her lungs. At the moment she didn't care if she ever figured it out, only that she felt it surround her, cover her and most importantly never leave her.

# Chapter Seven

ဢ

Ravid smiled in triumph. Zeva still slept in his bed and the sun was already up. It was still early but the slow rise and fall of her chest bore witness to the fact that they had worn her out.

That fact satisfied him greatly. His cock went hard as he lingered over her nipples. Zeva's little rose-tipped breasts made his mouth water as he passed a hand over the window screens to keep the room dark. Keenan depressed a few numbers into the temperature controls before he too ran his eyes over their sleeping mate.

They both headed towards the door curtain on silent feet. Overwhelming Zeva's body was only one part of the battle to winning her. The two men continued down the stairs as they embarked on the mission that would secure Zeva in their lives. She would not leave their protection if her studio weren't there for her to go to.

Their maroon coats caught the morning light as the people they passed fell out of their way. Firm resolve covered their faces and determination silently cleared a path for them.

\* \* \* \* \*

The chime from her communications terminal woke her. Zeva sat up as she fought against the bedding. The sheets were all cool telling her she had slept alone for at least an hour.

Scanning the room, she didn't find a trace of Ravid or Keenan. Disappointment crossed her mind and she couldn't stop the twist of unhappiness it created in her heart.

It was a silly idea but she wanted to see them this morning. Just why, she wasn't sure and as Zeva reached for her communications terminal, she decided she didn't want to find out either. It was just possible that a little mystery was a good thing between binding mates. Ravid and Keenan could keep their male arrogant ideas quiet and she wouldn't feel the need to battle with them…very often.

Zeva smiled at her own thoughts. Maybe that was a little oversimplified but learning to live with each other might be worth her time to work out their differences. Warriors and females were different. She couldn't expect Ravid or Keenan to understand her until she gave them the chance.

A message from her mother brightened the terminal as it chimed for attention on a nearby table. A frown marked her face as Zeva considered her mother's words. She had left a meeting place for her to come to in just an hour. Zeva knew the small lake that lay on the edge of the female grounds. She would only make the meeting if she hurried because it lay completely on the other side of the Judgment grounds and across her own family's warrior grounds and then onto the female grounds that were attached to the Sinlar household.

Paneil had never spoken of the place but it must have some significance to her binding day. There was no other reason for her mother not to greet her right here.

Zeva hurried through her bath as she considered Ravid's warning. She was wise enough to see the wisdom in staying on Judgment grounds. There were details to linger over but she could not resist their union any more than she could stop breathing.

She laughed as she looked at her reflection. Love didn't listen to common sense. She might try to impose logic onto her feelings but the emotions weren't going to heed anything but what her heart craved.

Zeva sobered as she looked around the room. Her memory replayed the night before and the determination that lived in both Ravid's and Keenan's eyes. She was not alone in the turbulence of deep need. Was that love? Well, whatever it was, they needed each other because separation tore at her soul.

Casting her eyes at the terminal, she moved towards the curtain. She would have to tell her mother that they had to meet on Judgment grounds until Helmut and Craddock were dealt with. She might not like that fact but Zeva wasn't foolish either.

Sometimes pride had to bend to common sense even if love didn't!

\* \* \* \* \*

"Did you kill her?"

A harsh grunt hit the morning as one warrior turned to his companion with a frustrated look on his face. "That would defeat our purpose."

"There is blood running down her face."

The first male looked at Zeva's crumpled body and shrugged. "Better her blood than mine. The bitch knows how to fight."

"True." Helmut knelt down and dragged their victim over his shoulder by her arm. He stood back up and glanced at her mother. Paneil's eyes were filled with pain as she pulled her broken leg to her chest. She cradled the injured limb as tears flowed down her cheeks. Helmut smirked at her growing horror as he settled Zeva's unconscious body over his shoulder. "Tell Ravid and Keenan their mate will not want for a cock in our care. We will use her body well and very often. Tell them I will teach her to call us master."

Paneil stuffed her hand into her mouth as a scream tried to erupt from her heart. The two males leered at her as the one named Craddock squeezed Zeva's unprotected bottom. Hatred blazed from their eyes as they smirked at her helpless body before turning towards their transport.

Once engaged, they lifted off the ground and sped away at top speed. Paneil searched the deserted area with desperate eyes before setting her teeth into her bottom lip and rolling onto her stomach.

She would crawl until she found help! Pain spiked through her leg as she moved and she cursed with words her children didn't know she knew.

"I will watch your bodies burn." Tears trailed down her checks as she dug her fingers into the soil. She had heard the whispers about dishonorable males but never thought to encounter any.

Paneil whimpered as she pulled her body forward. "My daughter will stand by my side as we watch your bodies burn!"

\* \* \* \* \*

"Bring them in here now!" Jett could have laughed if the matter wasn't so grave. His mother, who always smiled, was roaring at the top of her lungs. Medical attendants scurried out of her room as he walked in.

"Jett! Where are my sons-in-law?" Jett couldn't speak. Rage engulfed his brain as he tried to see his gentle mother beneath the blood and grime that covered her. She violently shook her head as a medical master tried to relieve her pain with a drug.

"No, I need my brain right now! Where are they, Jett?" Tears dropped down her cheeks as she moved and her body jerked with pain, but Paneil aimed her eyes at him and hit the side of her medical bed. "Where are my sons-in-law?"

"On their way." Jett didn't think it wise to correct his mother. Ravid and Keenan weren't bound to Zeva, at least not yet. His mother didn't seem to see a little detail like a public ceremony as any reason to not consider the two men her daughter's mates. Truthfully, he had seen the proof himself.

"Tell them to hurry up!"

The door dissipated in a shower of sparks as Ravid came through it too fast. Keenan was a half step behind him and Jett ended up pushed against a wall as the room filled with Judgment officials. They skidded to a halt as they got a look at Paneil, and his mother hit her bed with all her strength.

"Get moving! Haven't you ever seen a dirty female before?" Action was instant. A witness was never asked what happened, a memory seeker would view the crime through a psychic link. Paneil offered no resistance as one of the officials sat next to her bed and gently took the sides of her face in his hands. Horror played across his mother's face as she lived through each moment of being attacked once again.

"Now find my daughter." Paneil's strength appeared to flow out of her with the memory. She reached for Ravid and Keenan as her face lost its color. "Bring her back, my sons."

* * * * *

Pain woke Zeva. An odd mixture of pain coming from different parts of her body. Her head ached so bad she was sorry she even woke up. It felt like a knife was stuck down the back of her brain. Her arms hurt too and she opened her eyes just a tiny bit to look at her wrists. They were stretched out above her head and tied to a large hoop set into the wall. Her shoulders ached from her body weight that had simply hung while she was unconscious. Zeva straightened her legs to relieve the pressure only to discover that one ankle bitterly complained.

And she was completely naked.

"Her bones show." A pair of brown eyes raked over her skin as the scruffy-looking male took a huge swallow from a goblet. "I like my females to have curves."

"As long as her cunt is wet, who cares?" A second male walked across the room and took a long look at her nude form. Zeva stared straight back at him. There was one thing her time on Earth had taught her—never let scum see you respond. His eyes simmered with hatred as he brought them up to hers. "Hello, Zeva, I am Craddock. But you will call me only master."

Her eyes went large with horror because she just couldn't contain the telltale display. Craddock snickered and reached for her breast. Her stomach twisted with nausea as he squeezed it and pinched the nipple. His fingers felt dirty on her skin and her feet itched to kick him away from her body.

"Go on, Zeva, fight me. I like that. I hope you struggle when I get ready to fuck you. Ravid and Keenan have enjoyed taking away my life and now, I'm going to repay the favor by taking something away from them."

The goblet went smashing into the wall as Helmut moved across the floor to stand in front of her. "Let's fuck her before we cut her hair off. I want it to be full of my seed when we send it to them Judgment officials."

Craddock reached for her hands and cut the bindings. He clamped his hand around one of her wrists and dragged her away from the wall with a powerful jerk. This male might be Alcandian but he was not a warrior. He used his full strength on her, uncaring of the pain or injury it might inflict. "Fine with me, hair makes a good handle but I want to send Ravid and Keenan their mate's hair."

Zeva stumbled across the room as her mind frantically tried to think. It was a dirty, rundown room and her ears didn't hear anyone nearby. Taking on both males was not a very good idea. She was confident she could injure one but the second would not let her fight only one at a time.

A table broke her fall as her body slammed into it. Pain smashed into her belly as her hands went to keep her head from hitting the hard surface. At the last second Zeva let her arms fold and her forehead hit that table. A loud crack came from the impact before she let her body go limp and roll to the floor. She grasped at her control as she forced her body to lie like a broken doll on the floor. She wanted to fight but there was more than one way to defeat an enemy.

Craddock cussed and kicked her ribs. Zeva flopped over and fought the urge to hit him as he leaned over her. He slapped her face and she let the motion carry her head away from him, her hair flipped over her face giving her a shield to hide behind. He cussed again before standing up.

"What? You don't want her first?" Helmut sounded excited by the idea. Clearly he ended up second in line most of the time.

"I told you, I like a good fight." Craddock cussed again as he moved away from her body. "It's no fun to fuck a body. We'll wait until she wakes up."

"Guess she isn't all that strong." Helmut sounded disappointed as his voice got further away. "But she is just a female. I never understood why some of them try and learn defense arts. Waste of good time."

Minutes slowly ticked by and Zeva forced her body to remain still. A crash from the lower floor gave her a burst of hope and she opened her eyes just a slit. Afternoon light fought its way through the window curtains. She rolled over and onto her feet in a smooth motion that told her exactly how valuable her training was.

At that moment it was all that stood between her and Helmut and Craddock. A smile lifted her lips. She would win. Her hair would not be used to torment her mates, even if she had to kill to prevent it.

\* \* \* \* \*

Rage could control a man. Ravid let the emotion seep into every cell in his body as he searched the spot where Paneil's memory led them. His anger was more self-directed than aimed at Helmut and Craddock. Zeva was his mate, protecting her was his duty.

Especially from deviants.

"You cannot shoulder this blame, Ravid." Greer took Ravid's harsh look and refused to back down. "Even I would not have considered a deviant using a female's mother to trap her."

Greer was joined in that opinion by the Judgment officials who surrounded them. Ravid snarled softly and looked over the gravel lakeshore once again. There was nothing to find. Just the tracks from Helmut's and Craddock's boots mixed with the smaller ones of Zeva and Paneil. They had struck the women quickly and left just as fast.

Her communications terminal combination wasn't hard to get. Luring her mother to the spot as well was the hardest part. Craddock wanted Ravid to know who held Zeva. This was personal revenge and Ravid felt his rage burn even hotter as he faced the fact that it would not be over quickly.

Craddock wouldn't let him and Keenan off so lightly. The deviant held the one thing that could make him and Keenan bleed. No society was perfect, there were members who disagreed with the laws of their community. Craddock and Helmut saw themselves as true warriors—nothing would convince them otherwise.

Keenan turned to face him as their thoughts mingled. Pure male determination flooded the link between them as Keenan curled back his lips and growled. Ravid snarled in return.

It was time to kill.

\* \* \* \* \*

Zeva moved through the upper floor on silent feet. The chambers were in disrepair, some of the window screens completely off letting the elements in. Sounds drifted up from the lower floor letting her know that for the moment, Craddock and Helmut thought she was broken. But the lights had worked in the chamber she was tied up in, so there was still a main computer operating in the structure.

Looking out an open window, her eyes found nothing but unkempt grounds. There was no one to appeal to for help and the communications terminals in this chamber were blank and useless. Listening carefully, Zeva moved towards the next chamber. She was still naked but didn't waste her freedom on finding clothing. Craddock and Helmut would rip any covering off her body if they caught her so the effort was a waste of time.

What she needed was a functioning communications terminal! One little touch from her hand and it would instantly report her location to Ravid and Keenan. She was certain of that. Alcandar communications lines were all linked through Judgment control. If Judgment officials were looking for you, your handprint was tagged in the main computer lines. You could not even order a platter of food without it reporting back to Judgment control.

A set of stairs lay in front of her now. Zeva contemplated the added risk of descending to the main floor. The scent of food drifted up, tempting her to seek a working terminal on the bottom floor. She battled with the decision. Males such as Craddock and Helmut would kill her without hesitation. That truth sickened her but she forced herself to think about it. Her assumption that Alcandar was safe had led her to this moment when life could end so quickly.

Zeva tightened her resolve. Ravid's and Keenan's faces flashed through her memory, and the feeling of lying between them. She needed to feel that again! She had never been so acutely alive as she was when they were next to her. Getting back to them was worth the risk of going down those stairs.

Zeva listened to the sounds of her captors as she crept down those steps. She knelt down to make her body smaller as she neared the bottom. More noise filled the main eating area as the two males activated an entertainment screen. Zeva moved across the doorway as they aimed their attention at a sporting event.

Her reward awaited her a second later. A lit communications screen sat on the wall as she pressed her body against the wall. Grime coated the stone surface, making her

*Mary Wine*

skin itch. Zeva forced her hygiene concerns aside and pressed her hand against the terminal. A small beep registered acknowledgment before she slipped into the kitchen of the main floor.

Foul smells came from the food service area and it was a disaster. Apparently Helmut and Craddock lived exactly like the animals they were. Rotten food decorated the preparation counters and insects milled around.

"Craddock!" Helmut roared over the balcony and the entertainment unit went silent. "She's gone!"

Craddock cussed as the floor above her head shook under Helmut's running steps. Zeva swung her eyes around the kitchen, searching for any place to hide. She bent her knees and flattened her body against one of the center preparation tables. The ceiling shook as both males ran through the chambers looking for her. The sounds bounced off the walls in a confusing jumble making it impossible to determine where they were.

Light glittered off a knife and her hand reached for it without hesitation. It was a cutting knife, not a weapon, but the edge looked sharp to her desperate eyes. A strange sense of calm settled on her brain as she listened to the house go silent. They were hunting her now, stalking her within the walls like scavengers.

Zeva tightened her grip and hunched lower. Her eyes watched the shadows as she waited for a tiny little sound to give her a target. Craddock and Helmut had made one miscalculation.

She would not act like prey.

# Chapter Eight

**ဢ**

"She could be dead."

Greer's voice was controlled but the scene around him wasn't. Maroon-clad warriors battled against their own kind as Ravid and Keenan were held back by their comrades. Greer cast a long look at his communication bracelet and studied the information.

"Let me go, Osher." Keenan's voice was a low sound of warning. Osher looked at Greer before he let Keenan go. The warrior holding his opposite arm immediately stumbled back as Keenan flexed his shoulders. Rage burned from his eyes as he shot the warriors holding Ravid a warning look. Ravid took a long look at the information being displayed by his communication link. He shot Greer a hard look before reaching for a disintegration weapon.

"It matters not, I am going. This will end today." Ravid scanned the group of Judgment officials but no one protested his decision. Keenan moved beside him as Ravid caught sight of Amin.

His sister-in-law stood watching him with her son standing on a bench so that the child could clearly see. Amin's eyes were hard as she offered a single nod of her head.

"Let's go get our mate." Keenan's words were soft as he cast a look at Ravid. Burning in his eyes was a rage that demanded blood. It was a need that had driven them both for too long. Today they would come back with blood on their hands or they would be dead.

Primitive…hard…maybe even animalistic, but it was a warrior's way.

\* \* \* \* \*

Zeva felt her body shift into the tight control that she had lived with on Earth. It was an odd distortion of life where your emotions turned off and the instinct to survive rose to the top of your brain. Nothing mattered but ensuring that her lungs filled and her heart beat. She would do anything to ensure it. Her fingers grasped the knife handle and found the weapon comforting. It was one more little insurance that death would not take her without a struggle.

Her nose caught a faint smell drifting past. Her skin itched as she recognized it on some deep level. The few moments of captivity and helplessness were etched into her memory along with that scent.

A soft step hit her ears a second before the lights brightened. Zeva surged up from her hiding place and sliced through the air with her knife. Helmut's eyes rounded with surprise as the blade cut through his neck. His lips moved but she had cut the flow of oxygen from his lungs, rendering him silent in those last seconds of life.

The deviant fell back as Zeva tightened her grip on the handle. It was slick with blood and the metallic scent satisfied her need to survive. Helmut's eyes never closed. His body fell on the floor as his blood flowed out of his cut throat. Zeva looked at the body without remorse, instead all she felt was a surge of hope that she might have earned the right to live with her deed.

"You bitch." Cradock's face was distorted by rage. He looked at his fallen companion as his lips twisted with grief. "I'm going to send your body back to Ravid and Keenan in little pieces." His eyes burned as he lifted a finger. "And I'm going to make sure you live while I butcher you!"

His fist landed on her wrist and the knife went flying across the room. Pain raced up her arm as Zeva spun in a circle from the force of the blow. Craddock moved forward like a solid wall of death bearing down on her last moment of life.

Zeva kicked out her leg as she turned and hooked her heel as she caught sight of his head.

A sickening crack filled the air as her kick connected with Craddock's temple. Zeva turned with her kick and lowered her leg behind her in a perfect kicking position. Craddock stared at her with dazed eyes a second before his knees buckled and his body dropped towards the ground.

A flash of movement in the doorway made her jump around before her brain even registered who stood there. Ravid's hand held a weapon pointed at the spot Craddock had stood but his eyes were frozen on her. The muzzle of that disintegration rifle lowered as Zeva watched her own fist begin to vibrate. Her hand was covered in blood and she stared at it as the limb began to violently shake.

She didn't care about the two lives she'd taken. The bodies lay at her feet and all Zeva saw was Ravid's eyes. She could feel Keenan behind her as she let her hands drop to her sides. Ravid watched her with intense eyes, waiting for something that her brain couldn't seem to understand. The only thing she felt was a pressing need to be pressed between them. She had earned the right to feel their bodies next to hers and absolutely nothing else mattered.

"Take me home." Pain slashed across their mind-bridge as Ravid's lips tightened into a thin line. Keenan stepped back before touching her back, and she cast a look over her shoulder as emotion came spilling out of the walls she had locked it behind in order to survive.

Didn't they want her? The crimson blood coating her hand caught her eyes as Zeva shuddered with horror. Maybe they didn't want a mate who had taken lives. She lifted her eyes to Ravid and the tight mask he'd drawn his face into. She had to reach the man who was behind that taut control, because she wasn't sorry for her actions. "I had to do it... They were going to send you my hair...I had—"

Her words ended as Ravid crushed her with his arms. Keenan slammed into her back and she couldn't even fill her lungs as they smashed her body between their larger ones. Zeva frantically twisted between them, trying to touch and absorb the details of their bodies. The warm brush of breath on her neck, the beat of each male's heart beneath her fingertips. She needed to feel them!

Her lungs filled with their rich male scents and she felt her body rejoice. She had fought for the right to be close to them, even if it was just for one last time. They could renounce her, even impose penalty for taking life, but Zeva took a deep breath and straightened her back. She had no regrets. Deviants like Helmut and Craddock did not have the right to share her planet with her. She suddenly understood why warriors would pledge their lives to the Judgment ranks. Once your innocence was stripped away, how did you ever turn your back on the job that needed doing? She would never walk across the female ground with the same lack of care to attention.

And she certainly would never answer a summons without making certain it was sent by her family! Zeva lifted her head and looked into Keenan's topaz eyes. "I am not sorry. If that means I am a deviant, then I am."

Two grumbles of male displeasure hit her as the warriors surrounding them shot her a disbelieving look. "Defending yourself is not against the law, Zeva." Keenan suddenly looked down her body and shot a nearby warrior a harsh look. The man turned his back on her nude frame as Ravid released her in order to punch commands into his arm communicator. A little pop announced the arrival of whatever he had requested and Zeva found herself free of Keenan's embrace as Ravid wrapped her in a large sheet. The blood on her hands soaked right into the fabric, making her head spin in a dizzy circle. The surge of adrenaline was gone and her body was cheerfully releasing its grasp on consciousness. Slipping into deep oblivion beckoned to her like food to the starving.

Keenan picked her up and she sighed as her head found his chest to lean against.

* * * * *

"Mother!" Zeva surged up as she saw the transport heading for her mother's body. Every muscle drew taut but her eyes didn't show her the leering grins of Helmut and Craddock as they ran her mother down.

"Be at ease, *shihori*." Large hands stroked her face as Zeva tried to look at Keenan. She needed to see his face, just to assure herself that it was him.

But the chamber was dark, so all she saw was shadow. But it was Keenan. Zeva knew his scent, her skin confirmed that it was his hands smoothing over her cheeks. She knew his touch and how it differed from Ravid's. It wasn't something she could explain, only feel. Keenan's emotions touched hers and mingled in a stream of intimacy that fed her starving soul.

But she needed more. "Where is Ravid?"

Keenan threaded his fingers through her hair and inhaled her scent before answering. Relief surged through their mind-link before she caught just a hint of a smile lifting the corners of his lips. "He will be here shortly. First you need to dress."

The room brightened as Keenan moved away from her. Zeva lifted her hands to see her skin was clean. Even her fingernails were scrubbed free of every last hint of red. She lifted her hand and didn't even catch an odor of blood.

"I am amazed you did not wake during your bath. I confess I thought our mothers were going to peel your skin away with all their scrubbing." Keenan held a pair of her pants out but wouldn't let her take them. Instead he insisted on helping her dress.

Zeva looked at her hands again and rolled her eyes around to him. "You stayed?" Bathing was a female ceremony. Modesty did rise up as she thought about Keenan or any warrior being in the chamber while she bathed. That was not done on Alcandar!

Keenan grinned at her before holding out a jacket. "Someone had to hold you while you slept, *shihori*." His eyes

145

flashed with the endearment as Zeva froze in place just to savor the sound of that Alcandian word. Add to that the rich tone of Keenan's voice and she was completely content.

Ravid pushed the curtain aside and Zeva couldn't stop the smile her lips aimed at him. His face was a stone mask that twisted her stomach. Keenan's hand landed firmly on her back as a second team of warriors followed Ravid into their chamber. The fingers on her back made a soothing motion as a third warrior also walked into the room.

Her breath lodged in her throat as they considered her with serious eyes. Zeva held her chin high—she still wasn't sorry. The only thing she lamented was the fact that there needed to be Judgment officials because deviants existed.

The warriors suddenly moved and she was certain her heart froze. Their heads nodded with respect, stunning her. They swung her right arm across their chest to strike the top of their fist against their shoulder. On Alcandar, there was no higher praise from Judgment warriors.

Tension flowed out of her like ice that had been tossed into an open flame. Her knees wanted to buckle as a sigh escaped her lips. Ravid's eyebrow rose with confusion as he crossed the room to search her eyes with his dark ones.

"What were you expecting, Zeva?"

Ravid caught her chin as his mind mingled with hers...searching through her tattered emotions. She was too tired to care what he saw, relief still flowed so freely from the fact that she had awakened in Ravid and Keenan's chamber.

*Their chamber.*

"I am sorry, *ruthima.*" His eyes burned with guilt. Zeva gasped with horror as she watched Ravid shoulder the blame for her abduction. She grabbed his forearm when he moved to turn and grabbed and handful of his uniform top.

"It was not your fault." Zeva hissed each word in a louder tone. The last one was loud enough to shake the window coverings. Ravid's face flushed with pride and stubborn denial of her words. Zeva dug her fingers into the fabric covering his chest and heard a faint ripping sound as she dragged his head down towards hers. "Fate makes a lot of choices that we don't like."

Ravid's eyes widened as he listened to his own words. Zeva let his uniform go and balled her fingers into a fist. "I'd be happy to beat it into your thick skull. You two might not like it but I can look out for myself sometimes."

Ravid leaned down to whisper next to her ear. "And I will always argue with you."

"I hope so." Keenan raised an eyebrow at her words and Ravid did as well.

Greer cleared his throat. Ravid turned around abruptly as Keenan stepped up completely behind her. His hands landed on her shoulders in a solid motion of comfort.

"Mayhaps, we best finish this." A small smile betrayed his enjoyment before Greer stepped forward. Keenan leaned over her shoulder and spoke calmly near her ear.

"Greer, will observe your abduction before shifting it."

"No." The word came out of her lips before Zeva really understood what she objected to. Ravid shot her a confused look as Keenan's hands tightened on her shoulders. "Observing is fine, but I do not want it forgotten."

"Why?" Both her mates demanded that together. Greer looked at her with open astonishment. Ravid cupped her chin as his dark eyes cut into hers. "Zeva, there is no need for you to suffer with the memory."

But there was. Zeva felt each of Ravid's fingers along her jaw and noticed the stark difference between that touch and the one that Craddock had used on her. In that difference she finally understood why Ravid and Keenan were her mates. It went beyond the sexual fire and into the pure bliss of their connection to one another.

Keenan leaned over her ear. "The nightmares will be gone. Do not insist on keeping them."

"I have to." Zeva shook off their hands and stepped toward Greer. "I'll explain it to you once this is finished."

Keenan listened to his knuckles pop as he tightened his hands into fists. He wasn't sure if he could survive long enough to hear Zeva's explanation.

"It is shock speaking." Ravid growled around his words as they both flinched. They could not see what Greer witnessed through Zeva's eyes but the sickly pallor of her face as she relived her ordeal tormented them from their viewing spot. Endless moments of pain stretched them as Zeva's horror and desperation bled across their mind-link. Their comrades stood between them and Greer forcing Keenan and Ravid to let the investigation finish.

Greer grunted and stood up. "I am satisfied." The warrior left on silent feet a second before Zeva flew across the chamber. She jumped into the bathing pool with her clothes on as her body shuddered with horror.

It was just a memory! Zeva reached for that idea as her brain tried to yank her back into the nightmare. Nausea twisted her stomach as she swore she smelled the sickly scent of fresh blood. It was all over her! She had to get it off her skin!

"Zeva! Stop!" Ravid caught her body and crushed it within his embrace. Zeva thrust her hands against his embrace and slipped out of his hold.

Zeva submerged herself in the water and then thrust her body up. She shook the water off as she came face-to-face with Ravid and Keenan. They glared at her and she didn't mind the frustration, but the pity raised her temper.

"I am fine," she announced. "Better than fine, I am home."

A last shiver shook her body and Keenan snorted at her statement. "You need to let Greer shift that nightmare."

Ravid nodded agreement and Zeva reached for the buttons holding her soaking wet jacket on. A naughty smile lifted her lips. Life with Ravid and Keenan was never going to be smooth. Who could have ever thought that might be viewed as a positive aspect of their relationship? "I consider it an interesting gift."

"A what?" Zeva wasn't certain who said it louder. She was sure the eating hall below must have shook.

Zeva pulled her jacket off and tossed it onto the side of the pool. Ravid and Keenan frowned at her as they both battled to keep their eyes on her face instead of her bared breasts. She wanted to tempt them. She needed to watch the way their eyes moved over her body, not simple lust but driven by more than just the desire to fuck.

"They taught me something." It was horrible but true. Zeva looked at her warriors and saw everything that Helmut and Craddock hadn't been. Her eyes drank in the details. "I really thought I could live without you."

Zeva climbed from the pool and pushed her wet pants down her legs. "I can't. They showed me what selfish lust is and I don't ever want to forget the difference." Her eyes settled on the maroon coats as she smiled. "And I never want to forget that there is a reason for all of your rules for me."

Ravid caught her because he just couldn't contain the urge to touch her any longer. Zeva moved into his embrace with ease, letting him mold her to his body without resistance. Her scent filled his lungs as her breasts pressed against his chest. Keenan joined their embrace and Ravid shook with the pure perfection of it.

Zeva traced his chest with her fingertips, making him groan. The way she touched him sent fire coursing through his blood. She would trail those little fingers over each ridge on his chest and then sigh. It was the most basic form of compliment. There was no way to fake the delight simmering in her eyes as she touched his body. His next breath drew the hot smell of arousal into his head and his cock thickened in response.

Perfection. Zeva moved slightly so that her body moved against both warriors. Yes, she was right where she belonged. Keenan stroked her shoulders as Ravid's growl filled her ears. Their scents told her they were strong and the close embrace let her feel the twin erections just waiting for her to enjoy.

Lifting her chin she caught Ravid's eyes. They flashed blue electricity at her as his mind began to bridge with hers. Keenan leaned over her shoulder to draw a deep breath. His chest rumbled against her back as she felt his cock harden even further.

"Make love with me." Her words sounded desperate and maybe she was. Zeva didn't know or care. All that mattered was making a memory that would shame the one Craddock had left on her body.

Keenan chuckled in her ear and lifted her from her feet. He spun her in a wide circle before letting her body bounce on the bed. He stood just mere inches from the bed as his fingers unfastened his uniform. Zeva's breath caught in her throat as she watched him shrug out of it. Removing the maroon jacket didn't change the warrior that he was.

She saw that now. Noticed the honor that made up both warriors. It would drive her insane from time to time but tonight she would let them treat her like their mate.

Her skin grew hot as Ravid joined Keenan in disrobing. Ravid was more blunt in his motions. Raw desire spilled from his eyes as he lingered over her nipples. Zeva felt her passage flooding as she watched his eyes latch onto her nipples.

Ravid stopped before entering the bed and thrust one huge arm out to stop Keenan. His dark eyes moved over her nude body before he lifted them to her face. "Do you intend to bind with us, Zeva?"

Her pride didn't even bother to raise a protest. Her body needed them so much that the details of their lives would have to wait until desire had been fed. "Yes. But that doesn't mean I'm going to obey you. I'm not giving up my studio."

Twin smiles appeared on both warriors' faces as Zeva frowned. There was a little too much self-satisfaction in those expressions. Ravid fell on her in a second, making her gasp. His body weight didn't even hit her before he was rolling across the bed and taking her with him. "Enough talk."

Keenan hit the bed as Ravid rolled back over her and cupped one of her breasts. "Agreed." Zeva arched her back so that her breast pressed against Keenan's palm. Pleasure moved down her body to the twisting ache forming in her passage. Ravid moved down her body laying a row of kisses as he went. Keenan's arm moved to her opposite breast and cupped it, forming a barrier with his arm that pressed her back to the bed. It was a light hold but one that could so quickly become strong.

Ravid pushed her thighs open with his body as he lingered over her bare mons. He took a deep breath before opening his eyes to look at hers. "Aye, *ruthima*, I confess I enjoy the communication of the flesh far better than words."

Because he would win! Zeva surged up from the bed but Keenan pressed her back down. He leaned forward and caught a nipple with his lips. Zeva gasped as heat spiked through her breast and across to its twin. The other nipple tightened even further, begging for Keenan's hot mouth on it.

Ravid watched his companion with hungry eyes before he pushed her thighs wide. His breath hit her bare sex a second before he trailed his tongue along her open slit.

Climax took her that simply. Pleasure rippled through her sheath and up her spine. Ravid gently rubbed her clit as he watched her face. The pleasure left behind a deep hunger. Her passage ached to be full. She could feel the empty space inside her and it made her desperate. The desire filling her head from both warriors twisted and combined until nothing made any sense but the need to mate.

Keenan lifted his head and stared into her eyes. It was like looking into a mirror. His desire blazed as brightly as hers and Zeva reached for one of the hard cocks she craved. Keenan's eyes narrowed to slits as his breath hissed between his clenched teeth. She stroked the head before tightening her fingers around his length.

But it wasn't what she wanted. She wanted that cock thrusting deep inside her. Ravid pushed a single finger into her passage and she moaned with need. Her emotion shot across into both her mates and Ravid looked up her body with hard eyes. There was nothing playful about that look. It was completely male and Zeva looked to her side to find Keenan's eyes blazing as well.

She lifted her hand towards Ravid. He didn't disappoint her. Her pushed back onto his haunches and lifted her hips. One second she was poised on the tip of his cock before he pulled her onto it. Her passage eagerly grasped him as Zeva sat up and held onto his shoulders.

Keenan moved up behind her as Ravid lifted her and let her slam back down his length. He growled as she moaned but a soft cry hit the night as Keenan pulled the checks of her bottom apart. Ravid held her steady as Keenan applied a smooth lubricant to her back entrance.

Zeva wanted it. She needed both of them and she tightened her hands on Ravid's shoulders as Keenan's cock nudged her back entrance. The anal plug they had stretched her bottom with, left her relaxed for Keenan. His cock pressed forward and held as the head penetrated her body.

"I crave it too, Zeva." Keenan's voice was every bit as rough as Ravid's normally was. His hands pulled her bottom open wider as he pulled his cock from her and then thrust deeper into her. "The three of us together. Take me, *shihori*, let me fill you."

"Yes." Her voice was a firm demand. Zeva curled her fingers into Ravid's shoulders and he hissed. Keenan pressed deeper into her as Ravid lifted her off his cock. A moan escaped her as Keenan thrust completely into her bottom. Her back passage ached as Zeva struggled to relax. Keenan pulled free and Ravid thrust deeply into her.

The sensation was amazing. Zeva couldn't stop the little moans that rose from her. Ravid lifted her off his cock and Keenan thrust deeply into her bottom and then Keenan pulled his cock free and Ravid thrust deeply into her. They worked her body without granting her the one thing she craved the most.

"Together!" She hit Ravid's shoulder as she tried to push her hips down onto his cock. Climax shimmered just out of reach, tormenting her with its image, so close yet impossible to reach on her own.

"Yes, Zeva, you will take us both!" Ravid pulled her onto his cock as Keenan thrust deeply into her bottom. She was filled completely, and shuddered as they worked their hard cocks in and out of her. Pleasure shot through every nerve she had as her clit throbbed and Ravid thrust harder into her tight passage. Keenan's hips slapped against her bottom as he drove every last millimeter of his cock into her.

Zeva didn't know who came first. Their minds bridged completely and pleasure reflected off each other's pleasure. There wasn't one body...there were three and Zeva found herself dragged into the vortex of swirling, mind-blowing pleasure. Nothing existed outside of that moment, only the three of them bound together and the pleasure that awaited true intimacy.

Both cocks pumped into her body as her passage clamped around them and tried to milk them. Her womb twisted as it caught the hot splash of seed and her head fell back against Keenan's shoulder as she clung to Ravid's shoulders.

Their hands smoothed over her skin as her fingers traced the harder ridges of masculine chests. Zeva let her eyes slide shut as they let their bodies drop to the surface of the bed.

*Their bed.*

# Chapter Nine

## ℬ

"I have a gift for you." Keenan stroked her hip as Zeva tried to dig up enough strength to open her eyes. Ravid was behind her, his hard body cradling hers and all she wanted to do was have Keenan join their embrace.

Everything else could just wait…wait until she savored each moment of this night. Thinking about a gift meant she had to decide if she wanted to accept it from Keenan and that would bring up tomorrow's pressing issue of binding.

It was so much better to just escape into the delight of being next to both men without the complication of reality. Zeva lifted her arms towards Keenan. The warrior shook his head and Ravid moved. His hands lifted her from the bed as he sat up and let her lean against his body.

Zeva's brain instantly struggled to burn off her slumber. Once again the two were working like a perfectly matched team. One luring her into relaxing as the other maneuvered her into compliance.

"Keenan…"

Keenan's hand covered her lips as Ravid's arms clasped around her hips to keep her in place. "You will like our gift, Zeva." The guarded look on Keenan's face didn't make her believe his words. He offered her a small communications terminal. The silver rectangle displayed a document that her eyes scanned.

"It is a new studio." Ravid's voice was low as she flipped to the next page of a lease agreement. "This is on Judgment grounds and larger than your current one."

"You will need the room, we don't have a female training studio nearby. Once Greer and the others get to talking, every

Judgment father in our community will be presenting his daughters for your instruction."

Seconds crawled by like days as Keenan waited. Ravid shot him a look over Zeva's shoulder as they waited for her to finish reading. Her eyes rounded as she found the termination of her current lease agreement. Her lips thinned as she took a deep breath.

"You should have asked me before doing this." Zeva's words sounded too happy for her own pride. She looked at Keenan and shook her head. "Even Judgment officials should learn to discuss things with their mates."

Ravid's arms tightened around her making her gasp. Keenan's face broke into a grin as he pressed a hard kiss onto her mouth. Zeva pulled her mouth away and glared at him. "Did you hear me?"

"Aye!" Keenan plucked the terminal from her hand and tossed it onto the table before he clasped the sides of her face with his hands. "You said you will bind with me, mate."

"You did." Ravid spoke against her throat as he trailed little kisses toward her bare shoulder. Zeva grumbled and held Keenan away from her with stiff hands.

"I mean it! Discussion will happen in this chamber, if I must beat it into your stubborn, Judgment official heads!"

Keenan bent her arms and kissed her. It was a kiss of demand but not harsh. Ravid's arms moved over her in strokes that made her skin tingle with delight. Zeva melted against them as she kissed Keenan back.

They could discuss things later.

* * * * *

"Awake Daughter! Get up Zeva." Paneil held her arms wide to hold Milena and Elpida back. Her mother smiled as Zeva jumped from the bed and came up in a fighting stance. She blinked the sleep from her eyes as her mother turned to look at Elpida.

"My daughter moves before her mind engages." Elpida's eyes were wide but glittering with enjoyment.

"I will remember that, Paneil." Elpida's eyes slipped down Zeva's bare body as Zeva relaxed and looked behind her. The bed was empty and it shimmered as the bedding disappeared and clean sheets arrived on the bed.

"Our sons are below and it is time to dress."

The doorway curtain moved as Amin entered the room. Zeva groaned. Alcandian binding day, it meant the entire female side of the family got to see you naked. She moved toward the bathing pool as the chamber filled with chatter. A silly smile covered her lips as she surrendered to the bathing help. Her face turned red as the women began discussing sexual technique. Sweet Amin shocked her the most.

"If Ravid is like his brother, he will like his seed sac squeezed as he comes. Make sure you use your whole hand and close your fingers all the way around it."

Amin laughed and pointed at Zeva. "If you could only see your face!"

Zeva didn't need to see it, her cheeks burned with a blush as she was groomed and dressed for her binding ceremony. Her binding robes were dark blue and shimmered with silver. Paneil proudly brushed out her hair that hung down her back.

The hall below would be full of her family and Judgment families. Zeva listened to the growing conversations drifting up and over the half wall that formed the inner wall of their chamber. The fact that today marked her complete journey into the secluded life of Ravid and Keenan's world didn't bother her. She couldn't walk away without tearing her heart from her chest. Neither could her intended mates. She grimaced slightly as she looked across the chamber at the new lease they had procured for her. It had cost the two warriors quite a sum to move her studio. But it was a working solution and she had to smile at the idea. The new studio lay just a hundred feet onto Judgment grounds. Her current students could cross to the studio and she would not be breaking Ravid and Keenan's requirement that she stay on protected grounds. But she wouldn't be hiding either. Zeva smiled and turned to face the waiting binding party.

"I am ready."

Her mother and mothers-in-law–to-be proudly led her down the walkway to her mates. Two Judgment officials stood waiting for her with their wide chests covered with the maroon uniform that clearly displayed to the population their dedication to duty. Pride lifted her chin as she saw them waiting for her.

Zeva lost interest in the words as Ravid and Keenan stole her attention. They were every inch warriors. Contained in those words was so much more than her childhood had taught her.

And if she was lucky, a lifetime together would be just as informative!

\* \* \* \* \*

"Leave me be, Ravid, I am hungry." Zeva glared at her mate as she shot a second heated look at Keenan. "I am going to enjoy this meal with our guests and you can just wait."

Ravid growled and Keenan echoed the sound but Zeva sat down at the table waiting for her and refused to retire with them. Bound a whole ten minutes and they already made demands.

"Daughter, enjoy your meal." Paneil moved up onto the raised dais that the binding mates' table sat on. The hall was full of maroon-clad officials and their mates. Food passed freely down the tables as laughter filled the air. Her mother's eyes sparkled with mischief as she looked at her new sons-in-law. "I claim the right of inspection."

The hall fell silent for one moment before it erupted into a cheer. Ravid and Keenan both flushed before their mothers appeared to lead them away. Paneil winked at Zeva before she took her time following. Ravid shot her a furious look and Zeva laughed at his fury. She sat down and lifted an eating utensil in response and Elpida pulled her son around the corner.

"I think I missed something."

Zeva gasped and turned to find Cole Somerton leaning against the dais. He winked at her before jumping up onto the platform with her. Zeva stood up to offer the human a hug. "All you missed was the stubborn ignorance that often surrounds binding fever. Trying to make sense of it leads to foolishness on both sides. As you say on Earth, 'Don't ask me how I know'."

"I see." Cole's face said he didn't understand but he slipped his eyes down her body and back up again. "You look good, Zeva."

"It's good to be home." And it was a relief to see the human standing on Alcandian soil. There was another little thing that Helmut and Craddock had shown her. Honor wasn't contained in the Alcandian genetic code. It was something that was either bred in the soul or not. Cole Somerton was a warrior and she was proud to share her homeworld with him.

"Welcome home, Cole, I'm proud to have you joined to my family."

Zeva sat down and offered an empty chair to Cole. He dropped into it as Jett took the one on the other side of Zeva. Home? He didn't know about that but it sure beat being a fugitive on Earth. The future was a thick swirling mass of uncertainty.

But tonight there was family and that wasn't bound by a person's birth planet...even if York wanted it to be.

\* \* \* \* \*

"You took your time."

159

Zeva smiled at Ravid as she balanced a tray of food on her forearm. Keenan lifted it away and pulled a piece of meat from it. He stuffed it in his mouth as he glared at Zeva for making them wait.

"You have no one to blame but yourselves. I think my mother likes you both." Keenan snarled through another bite of food and Zeva squealed as Ravid plucked her off the ground. It was easy to forget how much larger the warrior was than her. Yet he never hurt her and that was what allowed him to make her cry like a little girl when he lifted her like one. Trust. More than body, she trusted them both with her heart. Zeva caught his head between her hands and smiled down into his dark eyes. "I love you too."

Keenan pointed at her. "If I didn't love you, Zeva, I would have tossed your mother into our bathing pool. She enjoyed inspecting us."

"A little too much," Ravid snarled as Zeva kissed his lips.

"You had it coming." Zeva lifted a bit of food toward Ravid and pushed it against his lips to keep the warrior from muttering against her mother again. "You cannot deny it. One inspection deserves another."

Love wasn't dictated by any one tradition. It flowed through time and space surrounding male and female. The only rule was obedience and the chosen ones never argued with their fate.

# Also by Mary Wine

໕

A Wish, A Kiss, A Dream (*Anthology*)

Alcandian Quest

Alcandian Soul

Beyond Boundaries

Beyond Lust

Dream Shadow

Dream Specter

Dream Surrender

Ellora's Cavemen: Tales from the Temple III (*Anthology*)

Scarlet Stockings

Tortoise Tango

White Hot Holidays Volume 1 (*Anthology*)

# About the Author

ॐ

I write to reassure myself that reality really is survivable. Between traffic jams and children's sporting schedules, there is romance lurking for anyone with the imagination to find it.

I spend my days making corsets and petticoats as a historical costumer. If you send me an invitation marked formal dress, you'd better give a date or I just might show up wearing my bustle.

I love to read a good romance and with the completion of my first novel, I've discovered I am addicted to writing these stories as well.

Dream big or you might never get beyond your front yard.

I love to hear what you think of my writing:

Mary welcomes comments from readers. You can find her website and email address on her author bio page at www.ellorascave.com.

## Tell Us What You Think

We appreciate hearing reader opinions about our books. You can email us at Comments@EllorasCave.com.

# Why an electronic book?

We live in the Information Age — an exciting time in the history of human civilization, in which technology rules supreme and continues to progress in leaps and bounds every minute of every day. For a multitude of reasons, more and more avid literary fans are opting to purchase e-books instead of paper books. The question from those not yet initiated into the world of electronic reading is simply: *Why?*

1. ***Price.*** An electronic title at Ellora's Cave Publishing and Cerridwen Press runs anywhere from 40% to 75% less than the cover price of the exact same title in paperback format. Why? Basic mathematics and cost. It is less expensive to publish an e-book (no paper and printing, no warehousing and shipping) than it is to publish a paperback, so the savings are passed along to the consumer.

2. ***Space.*** Running out of room in your house for your books? That is one worry you will never have with electronic books. For a low one-time cost, you can purchase a handheld device specifically designed for e-reading. Many e-readers have large, convenient screens for viewing. Better yet, hundreds of titles can be stored within your new library — on a single microchip. There are a variety of e-readers from different manufacturers. You can also read e-books on your PC or laptop computer. (Please note that Ellora's Cave does not endorse any specific brands.

You can check our websites at www.ellorascave.com or www.cerridwenpress.com for information we make available to new consumers.)

3. *Mobility.* Because your new e-library consists of only a microchip within a small, easily transportable e-reader, your entire cache of books can be taken with you wherever you go.

4. *Personal Viewing Preferences.* Are the words you are currently reading too small? Too large? Too... ANNOYING? Paperback books cannot be modified according to personal preferences, but e-books can.

5. *Instant Gratification.* Is it the middle of the night and all the bookstores near you are closed? Are you tired of waiting days, sometimes weeks, for bookstores to ship the novels you bought? Ellora's Cave Publishing sells instantaneous downloads twenty-four hours a day, seven days a week, every day of the year. Our webstore is never closed. Our e-book delivery system is 100% automated, meaning your order is filled as soon as you pay for it.

Those are a few of the top reasons why electronic books are replacing paperbacks for many avid readers.

As always, Ellora's Cave and Cerridwen Press welcome your questions and comments. We invite you to email us at Comments@ellorascave.com or write to us directly at Ellora's Cave Publishing Inc., 1056 Home Avenue, Akron, OH 44310-3502.

erridwen, the Celtic Goddess of wisdom, was the muse who brought inspiration to story-tellers and those in the creative arts. Cerridwen Press encompasses the best and most innovative stories in all genres of today's fiction. Visit our site and discover the newest titles by talented authors who still get inspired - much like the ancient storytellers did, once upon a time.

## Cerridwen Press

www.cerridwenpress.com

*Discover for yourself why readers can't get enough of the multiple award-winning publisher*

*Ellora's Cave.*

*Whether you prefer e-books or paperbacks,*

*be sure to visit EC on the web at*
*www.ellorascave.com*

*for an erotic reading experience that will leave you breathless.*

CPSIA information can be obtained at www.ICGtesting.com
Printed in the USA
BVOW08s1840310114

343636BV00001B/97/P

9 781419 954061